Ines Allerheiligen

Sleeper Cell

Ines Allerheiligen

Sleeper Cell

Bibliographic information from the German National Library:
The German National Library lists this publication in the German National
Bibliography; detailed bibliographic data is available online at
http://dnb.dnb.de.
Impresses
English-language first edition June 2025
Copyright © 2025 Ines Allerheiligen
Cover design by Ines Allerheiligen

Publisher: BoD · Books on Demand GmbH, Überseering 33,
22297 Hamburg, bod@bod.de
Print: Libri Plureos GmbH, Friedensallee 273, 22763 Hamburg
ISBN (Print): 978-3-8192-8095-5

Mosul – 2015

The city groaned under the relentless midday heat. The air shimmered over the cracked asphalt streets, where small, deceptive puddles collected like liquid silver – merely an illusion, born of the heat. People had long since retreated to their houses, seeking shelter from the scorching sun. Even the shadows seemed dull and lifeless, as if the heat had robbed them of all depth. The shutters of most buildings were closed. The temperature had risen to a relentless 43 degrees Celsius this week. The sky stretched cloudless and leaden over the city, an endless, merciless blue, with no relief in sight. You could practically taste the dust on your lips. It settled on your skin, mixed with your sweat, and formed a thin film that was almost impossible to wipe away. The plants in the front gardens stood with drooping leaves, withered and brittle like old paper.

Mosul, the second-largest city in Iraq after Baghdad, lay on the western bank of the mighty Tigris River, which originated in eastern Turkey. Its waters carved through the landscape, winding through barren plains and fertile valleys before skirting the Syrian border and flowing further south. There, it joined the Euphrates, and together they flowed as a mighty river through the heart of Mesopotamia, finally disappearing into the Persian Gulf.

The Tigris River was the lifeblood of this city, but in the scorching heat of summer, even its waters seemed to flow more slowly. Powdery layers of dust settled along the banks, scattered in all directions by the wind.

Mosul, a city rich in history and diversity, was characterized by its numerous mosques, their minarets proudly rising into the sky. Particularly striking was the Great Mosque of Al-Nuri, whose ornate tower was a landmark of the Mosul skyline. It was a place of prayer, but also a symbol of cultural identity and architectural mastery.

With the discovery of oil in the 20th century, the city transformed rapidly. This newfound prosperity was reflected in the form of modern buildings that sprang up among traditional structures. Oil refineries sprang up and spread throughout the surrounding area. A new infrastructure emerged, with new roads, bridges, and utilities, to support the growing population and industry. But Mosul remained a city that had not forgotten its history. The old mosques, the bazaars, and the narrow streets continued to tell stories from past centuries.

But the peaceful diversity that once characterized Mosul had shattered. Many people had left the city in recent years. In June 2014, Mosul fell into the hands of the so-called Islamic State. The brutal conquest changed the city irrevocably.

Mosul was once a city of diverse cultures and faiths. Kurds, Yazidis, Arabs, Shiites, Sunnis, and Christians lived side by side here. Their languages and traditions shaped the cityscape and were each destroyed by the jihadist invasion.

Christians in particular suffered under the new rule. They were given a choice: either convert to Islam, leave the city, or be executed. The streets, once filled with lively commerce, became emptier. Houses stood abandoned, entire neighbourhoods seemed deserted. Since then, the strict rules of the so-called caliphate prevailed. Sharia law was enforced with iron severity, and life in Mosul changed dramatically.

Life in Mosul was now characterized by constant control and fear. There were rules and harsh punishments for everything. Men had to wear long beards—a symbol of supposed righteousness. If a beard wasn't long enough, a fine of 10,000 dinars followed. Clothing was also controlled: If trousers weren't short enough, there were ten lashes. But these rules were just the beginning. Cell phones were banned, as were the internet, cigarettes, photographs, hookahs, and music. Anything considered un-Islamic or that could threaten the rulers' control was rigorously suppressed.

But as is so often the case, the rules didn't apply to everyone equally. Foreign IS fighters enjoyed special rights. They were allowed to visit internet cafes, while the locals were completely cut off from the outside world.

The streets, once filled with voices and life, were now silent and tense. One wrong word, one inappropriate look, and punishment threatened, which only made things worse.

The cityscape had changed. The faces of the images in the city, even those of animals, had been painted over. The heads of sculptures in parks, museums, and public squares had been cut off. Only Allah was supposed to have the power to create creatures.

The new IS-controlled authorities levied a tax on everything. Anyone who couldn't pay it had to join the fight. The traditional textbooks in the schools were burned, and new textbooks were introduced. In these, the children learned about assembling weapons, how to operate them, how to drive a tank, and they watched videos of the beheading of infidels.

Aliya's family was among those who suffered particularly under the new regime. Their modest income was barely enough to meet the constant demands of the occupiers. Many families were able to use bribes or connections to keep their sons away from school, where the ideology of the so-called Islamic State was taught. But Aliya's family had neither enough money nor influential contacts.

So, they had no choice. Rais, the family's only son, had to go to school. He left home every day with a heavy heart, because the lessons no longer consisted of mathematics, history, or literature. Instead, hatred was preached, war was glorified, and obedience to the self-appointed leaders was demanded. Rais was a scrawny 14-year-old boy with large, fearful eyes. While his classmates already proudly displayed their first beards, which they had grown exactly according to the rules, only a small fuzz had formed on his upper lip. They called him *walid sarier*, or little boy. There were many boys in his class who were there against their will, but none suffered as much as Rais.

Aliya's family was not particularly large. Besides her brother Rais, she had two sisters. Muna, the eldest, was now twenty years old, while Mariam, at eighteen, was only two years younger. Aliya herself was the youngest in the family. She had turned sixteen in the spring. Muna and Mariam were already married and no longer lived at home. Their weddings had been simple but joyful occasions—celebrations full of laughter, music, and delicious food. Memories that felt like they came from another life. Now she lived alone in the house with her parents and Rais.

Despite the intense heat, Aliya wore an abaya and a niqab that morning. Only her large, almond-shaped eyes, the colour of dark emeralds, peered vigilantly through the narrow slit of the niqab, watching the cars struggling through the streets of Mosul in the heavy midday traffic. She had pulled black gloves over her hands. Aliya strictly adhered to the dress code that had been introduced since the Islamic State took over Mosul, and she also adhered to the new rules in other ways. She would have loved to go to school in Rais's place to learn everything about true Islam. But as a woman, she wasn't allowed to, and so she had to leave school last year and since then has been helping her mother with the housework.

Every night, when Rais was in bed, she secretly took his school supplies and retreated to the small pantry. There, she made herself comfortable behind the shelf of canned chickpeas and devoured the new books as if they were a great treasure. The words burned them-selves into her brain, and she didn't need to read them a second time. Rais had carelessly thrown the books onto the table. Aliya read the words he hated so much and couldn't understand why his rejection was so strong. Perhaps it was the constant fear of being watched and punished if he just thought the wrong thing. But she felt a deep peace and closeness to Allah when she read her brother's books.

Aliya continued to struggle through the heat. Each new step seemed harder than the last. The sun burned mercilessly from the sky, and her clothes clung un-comfortably to her skin.

On the next corner was a large fruit and vegetable market, Aliya's final destination for the day. When she arrived at the market stall where the family usually shopped, the vendor was already putting away some of his wares to close for the midday prayer.

"Can I have some more dates?"

Aliya looked shamefacedly at the street, avoiding the man's direct gaze.

"Of course, which ones would you like?"

"I'll take a kilo of the loose dates over there on the right," she pointed to a box of large dates. She always went to this market stall to buy dates. They were soft and exceptionally sweet. The whole family loved to eat these dates in the evening while her father recited the Quran.

The vendor took four handfuls and dropped the dates into a paper bag. Then he weighed them.

"There you go, exactly one kilo."

Aliya paid, said her goodbyes, and headed home. The muezzin had already begun the call to prayer, and she had to hurry to avoid missing the *zuhur*, the midday prayer. From the market, it was only a few minutes to her parents' house. Al Shabab Street was a narrow street lined with low houses with peeling plaster and iron gates. Her family's house stood out from the others, at least to Aliya. It was a beautiful house, not because of its size or splendour, but because of the sense of security it exuded. A small garden adorned the entrance area and wrapped around the house. It was just big enough for the family to keep some chickens and grow a few vegetables. Aliya loved working in the garden. She had planted beautiful flowerbeds right along the wall surrounding the garden. One half of the beds was planted with colourful flowers, around whose blossoms a variety of insects thronged in spring, and the other half was filled with tomatoes, chickpeas, beans, and a variety of herbs whose fragrance hung in the warm air.

Since the sisters moved in with their husbands' families, the garden had been her little kingdom. She fed the chickens and cleaned the coop. Growing vegetables wasn't always easy. Some days there wasn't enough water to irrigate the plants. Then they would dry out, or Aliya would harvest the vegetables when they were still very small, before they were no longer edible. The house was surrounded by a three-meter-high wall to protect it from the neighbours' view, especially from the men. This allowed Aliya to walk around the garden, work, or simply relax without wearing an abaya or hijab.

At the very back of the garden stood a small Arbor, hidden behind a gnarled olive tree. Two sturdy grape vines had twined themselves around the wooden structure over the years. Their tendrils, entwined like a natural net, almost completely enveloping the cottage. A small, narrow stone path wound directly from the house entrance. A white and a red grape cluster wound along each side of the Arbor.

In autumn, the Arbor transformed into a true paradise. The vines hung heavy under the weight of plump, juicy grapes, shimmering in the mild autumn sun. Aliya loved sitting here and plucking the sweet fruit directly from the vines. She only had to lift her head, and she could grasp the grapes with her mouth, almost as if she were in paradise.

The Arbor had many cushions to sit on, as well as pillows leaning against the walls. In the summer, the whole family would sit here and enjoy delicious chai, mate, or mocha, eat homemade pastries, and listen to the Quranic verses read aloud by her father. On the other side of the garden, where the sun shone the longest, Aliya had planted a small date tree last year. It was a delicate sapling, little more than a thin trunk with a few green leaves poking defiantly out of the dry earth. She had grown it herself, from the pits of the sweet dates she always bought at the market.

Many years would pass before the small date tree would bear its first fruit. She imagined herself one day sitting under the broad shade of her own date tree. The leaves would rustle gently in the breeze as she leaned against the trunk, her eyes half-closed, a small pot of steaming tea beside her, its aroma mingling with the warm air. And in her hand, she would hold sweet and soft, golden-brown dates from her own tree.

When Aliya arrived home, she hurried into the house. Her steps led her straight to the kitchen, where she quickly placed the fruit and vegetables she had bought at the market in the refrigerator. It was important to store everything quickly before the heat could spoil the fresh foods. After washing her hands and face with cold water, she went into the large living room. Her parents and Rais were already waiting there, ready for midday prayers. The room was simple but well-kept. Colourful rugs lay on the floor, and the light of an old oil lamp flickered faintly in one corner.

Aliya took her own prayer rug from the shelf, carefully spread it on the floor, and stood behind it. She felt the silence in the room, a peaceful silence that grew deeper with each breath. Together they bowed their heads in prayer and listened to the familiar words of their father.

After the prayer, her mother beckoned Aliya to come over. "Come, follow me into the kitchen," she said with a smile. Aliya looked questioningly at her mother as she continued.

"Today is a special day. We're expecting guests for tea."

"What kind of guests?" Aliya was surprised, because they usually only welcomed guests on the weekends. They always cooked days in advance, and everything was prepared to welcome them. But today was different. Her mother lowered her gaze, as if considering something, before answering in a low voice: "It will be your future husband. And his parents."

Aliya opened her eyes wide in astonishment and stared at her mother in disbelief.

"What? Who is this man?"

"You don't know him," her mother replied calmly. "Don't ask too many questions. This isn't the time. Quickly go upstairs to your room and get ready for your big day. I'll prepare everything for the guests."

Aliya ran up the stairs, her footsteps echoing softly in the quiet house. Her room was on the first floor. She had previously shared it with her two sisters, Mariam and Muna. But everything had changed in the last year. Muna had been the first to move out, right after her wedding. Mariam followed just six months later. Now Aliya was left alone in the large room that had once been full of laughter and conversation. It felt strangely quiet, almost empty. The room next door belonged to Rais. Her parents' bedroom was at the other end of the hall.

Aliya collapsed onto her bed, took a deep breath, and tried to collect her thoughts. No, she was neither afraid nor sad, for she knew the tradition by which a man was chosen for the daughters of families.

The man came with his parents to visit the family home of the woman he wanted to marry or whom his family had chosen for him. The daughter of the house served the tea and kept a low profile. This was the first contact between husband and wife. If her father agreed and considered the man a good fit for his daughter, and the man's family also agreed, everything would be prepared for the wedding. Those were the traditions, and she would accept them.

Aliya stood up and went into the small bathroom adjacent to her room. She washed her face and ran her fingers through her hair to comb it. For this special day, she chose her most beautiful abaya. A hint of excitement rose within her, accompanied by a feeling she couldn't quite identify. Joy? Nervousness? Maybe both. She was ready to meet her future husband.

After she finished, she sat by the window, which afforded a wide view of the garden. The flowers, the trees, and the gentle breeze blowing through the open window seemed to calm her. She reached for her Quran, opened it, and began to read a few verses in a whisper. The familiar words gave her comfort, helped her to collect herself and quietly enjoy the moment.

She waited for her mother to call her. Only then would she go downstairs to the living room to join the guests.

There was a soft knock at the door.

"Aliya? Are you ready?"

Aliya jumped up, kissed the Quran gently, and then carefully placed it back in its place. Her fingers touched the precious book with tenderness, as if she wanted to draw some comfort from it before facing reality. She opened the door and stepped out, the tension palpable in her body, but also a strange calm within.

"Yes, Mom. I'm ready," she said, almost whispering the words.

She followed her mother into the kitchen, where a tray was already waiting for her. It was a carefully prepared arrangement of teacups, spoons, and small, golden bowls filled with sweets. Aliya picked the tray with trembling hands and followed her mother into the parlour. As soon as she entered, she heard the faint murmur of voices. Her heart beat faster as she

took a step closer. She bowed her head, a sign of respect and shyness, and only cautiously let her gaze
wander through the gap in her veil. On one side of
the table sat a man. He was perhaps in his early 50s,
with thick, slightly wavy black hair that was well-
groomed. The grey caftan he wore was both elegant
and simple, and a scarf was artfully wrapped around
his head. Next to him sat a woman who also behaved
modestly. She had bowed her head and wore an abaya.
Aliya approached them slowly and offered them tea
and some sweets from her tray. Finally, she turned to
the young man sitting next to her father. Their gaze
met only briefly. He had dark brown eyes that re-
garded her shyly, yet at the same time with a warmth
that momentarily took her breath away. They were the
warmest eyes Aliya had ever seen - eyes that radiated
a quiet security - eyes in which she lost herself. He,
like his father, had black hair, but it was straight. His
hair hung just past his shoulders and flowed into a
well-groomed beard. He, too, wore a scarf around his

head and was dressed in a white caftan. He had fair skin and a slim build. When Aliya offered him tea, he accepted it, looked briefly into her eyes again, and then immediately turned back to Aliya's father.

Aliya sat on a stool next to the door, away from the table, and listened to the conversations. He had a calm voice and a refined way of expressing himself. Aliya liked it. His name was Isa; he was 31 years old and had studied medicine at the university in Mosul. He had spent the last year in England, working in a hospital in London. Aliya's father seemed very impressed with him.

After a while, Aliya went into the kitchen to make another pot of tea. When she returned to the living room, she heard her father say to Isa, "So we're agreed. The wedding will take place in two weeks so you can leave on time."

The two men shook hands, the wedding a done deal.

The last two weeks had flown by, and Aliya could hardly believe how quickly the time had passed. It felt like yesterday was the day her mother had told her about her future husband. There was a lot to organize. Aliya needed a visa, a wedding dress had to be sewn, and travel arrangements had to be made.

After Isa and his parents left the family home, she learned that she and her husband would be flying to London on the day of the wedding. Isa had secured a permanent position as an anaesthesiologist at St. Mary's Hospital in London's Paddington district. The apartment they would be living in was close to the hospital. While her husband went to work, Aliya would receive English lessons and learn everything about the culture and life in her new home.

The closer the wedding day drew, the more with-drawn Aliya became. It wasn't because of Isa; she liked him, even though she hadn't seen him since the day they met. Nor was it because she had to leave her parents' home. Rather, it was the thought that she and

Isa would be going to Europe, to London. To a country so different from her home. Europe had always seemed distant and unattainable to her. In the books Rais brought home from school, which Aliya loved, England was a land of unbelievers. They left no doubt that people in Western countries lived in sin and shame. They didn't pray to Allah; women openly displayed their bodies and their hair; they listened to music, danced, and entertained themselves in bars and clubs, loving luxury and extravagance rather than being content with the things Allah had intended for them.

The evening before the wedding, as Aliya was making the final preparations with her mother in the kitchen, she seemed so distracted that her mother confronted her about it.

"Aliya, you have become so quiet these past few days. Don't you like your future husband?"

Aliya looked at her mother, her eyes filling with tears.

"Yes Mother, I like Isa, very much. But the thought of us going to London to live scares me."

"Aliya, London is a very beautiful city," her mother said gently.

"Isa has told your father a lot about life there. The people are open and friendly. They will welcome you with open arms. You will learn a lot—a new language, a new culture. You will leave Mosul and be able to live freely, without the rules the Islamic State has imposed on us here."

"But I love my life here and I love the rules the Quran has imposed on us. I don't want to change, and I won't let anyone bend me. They won't accept me as I am."

"You are not alone, Aliya. You have your husband by your side. You will learn a lot and you will love life there, and now I don't want to talk about it any further. I won't tell your father about our conversation, and I don't want you to either. You must submit and follow your husband wherever he goes. Now go to your room and prepare for your big day tomorrow."

Aliya hadn't expected her mother to react so harshly and show so little understanding. She had been sure her mother would understand. From her room, she looked out into the garden, into her garden. The small date palm stood still in the moonlight. It didn't move a millimetre, even though a light breeze had started, which its narrow branches stirred tirelessly.

"I will be like my little date palm," thought Aliya. "Strong and fearless. Nothing will bend me."

She opened the window and whispered into the night: "Goodbye, my little date tree. One day I'll come back. Then I'll sit beneath you, drink tea, and snack on the dates you'll then bear."

She closed the window and felt a pleasant calm spread within her. She would never speak of this subject to anyone again.

London

Aliya's fingers gripped the back of her seat. The roar of the turbines filled her ears as the pressure on her chest increased. A tremor ran through the aircraft as the plane began to move across the runway. It got faster and faster. She was pressed into her seat and felt as if her breath was being taken away. She looked out the window and saw the landscape slowly tilting to the side. The world below her was shrinking rapidly, streets becoming thin lines, houses tiny dots.

"We're taking off," she thought.

She forced herself to take a deep breath and loosen her grip on the seatback.

It was her first flight. Isa, sensing her fear, placed a light hand on her arm.

"You don't have to be afraid. Once we reach cruising altitude, you won't even notice we're flying."

Aliya smiled shyly at her husband. Slowly, she calmed down. Isa radiated an unbridled confidence and calm, and to her surprise, Aliya was able to embrace it.

Just this morning, she and Isa had married, and now they were already on their way to London. She was flying to a new life, to a strange city, with a man she'd only known for a few hours. Since then, they'd exchanged little more than pleasantries. They'd chosen their words carefully and formally in every conversation.

Now she sat here, thousands of feet above the ground, between her new life and the home she'd left behind.

She'd allowed herself to be persuaded to wear only the hijab for the trip to London, even though she didn't like it. Without the niqab, she felt naked, vulnerable, as if any gaze could strike her unexpectedly. Her mother had convinced her otherwise.

"It will be easier, Aliya," she'd said.

"In London, people often don't understand our culture; it frightens them. Don't make it harder than it already is."

Her mother's words worried her. What kind of life would await her in London? Would she ever feel at home there?

The captain's voice came over the loudspeaker: "Dear passengers. We have now reached our intended altitude of 30,000 feet. The weather is sunny and calm. The flight time to London is seven hours and ten minutes, and we are expected to land at Heathrow Airport around 10 p.m. local time. I wish you a pleasant flight."

Aliya took a deep breath and dared to look out the small, round window. She saw many clouds and the rays of sunlight on the horizon. It was an infinity that fascinated her, and she felt closer to Allah than ever.

"This is beautiful, Isa."

"I know. I, too, was enchanted on my first flight. We can unbuckle our seatbelts now," he said, helping Aliya unfasten her seatbelt.

"Would you like something to drink or eat?"

"Later. I'm going to pray now. Is there a place to do that on the plane?"

"Yes, there is a prayer room."

Aliya stood up carefully and walked, at first a little unsteadily, but then with firm steps, to the room just before the cockpit.

It was a very small room, but it was large enough for one prayer. On the right side, right next to the door, a woman was already kneeling, deep in prayer, with a man next to her. Further ahead, two more men were praying. Aliya decided to choose the left side for herself. She carefully laid out her prayer things, closed her eyes for a moment to calm herself, and began her prayer. For the first time, she thought: Why hadn't Isa accompanied her to prayer?

When she was finished, she folded her prayer rug, stood up, and made her way back to her seat. For a brief moment, her eyes met those of the woman who had prayed beside her husband.

When she sat next to Isa again, she saw that he had already ordered food. In front of him was a tray with chicken, rice, and a small salad. He was still busy with his meal, while her tray of fresh salad was being served.

"Why aren't you praying?" Aliya asked quietly as she dipped her fork into the salad.

"I'll make up for the prayers later," Isa replied casually as he took a bite.

"You'll see, once we get to London, there will be different priorities, a different daily routine. You'll get used to it."

Aliya looked at him with a surprised expression as she chewed her salad. "But I don't want to get used to it," she thought resolutely. Even though life in London might challenge her, she would always stick to her duties.

Aliya spent most of the rest of the journey in silence. She stared out the window, where the clouds floated like soft cotton balls beneath the plane. The last few days had been so exhausting—the farewells, the packing, the endless preparations. At some point, as she remained lost in thought, fatigue overcame her, and she slipped into a deep, dreamless sleep.

She didn't awaken until the pilot made the landing preparation announcement. The passengers were supposed to fasten their seatbelts and return the seatbacks to their normal seating positions. Aliya blinked sleepily and sat up. Her eyes felt heavy, but the view out the small window immediately woke her up. Lights spread out below, like sparkling pearls.

"We're about to land, fasten your seatbelt," Isa said, glancing at her quickly as he tightened his seatbelt.

Aliya also reached for her seatbelt and clicked it into place. Her heart beat a little faster.

"Is that London below us?" she asked with a mixture of curiosity and nervousness.

"Those are just the suburbs," Isa explained, pointing out the window. "London is huge, big, full of life. You'll love it."

He smiled at her encouragingly, but Aliya could barely suppress her excitement. She wanted to believe she would like it, that she could settle in here. But a part of her couldn't stop thinking about what she'd left behind.

Heathrow Airport was huge, and Aliya felt overwhelmed by its vastness and hustle and bustle. The ceiling of the arrivals hall was high, the lights were bright, and all around her, people were bustling around. She sat down on a bench, put her bag next to her, and waited for Isa, who was standing at the baggage carousel, waiting for her suitcases. As she waited, she let her gaze wander around the arrivals hall. The hall was crowded with people—travellers in a hurry, greeters hugging each other. Everywhere there was conversation, the clatter of suitcases, and the murmur of announcements from the loudspeakers.

Suddenly, she noticed a face in the crowd. A young woman who turned directly toward her and gave her a slight nod. Aliya was surprised for a moment, but then she recognized the woman. It was the one who had prayed in the plane's prayer room. She returned the gesture and smiled back. The woman seemed to have noticed, and for a moment their gaze held. But then the man appeared at the woman's side, and together they disappeared into the dense crowd.

Aliya sat quietly, thinking about the encounter. It was strange to have recognized someone in this vast, unfamiliar city whom she had only recently seen on the plane.

She looked around again until she finally spotted Isa approaching her with her suitcases. She stood up and went to meet him, her thoughts still on the strange woman.

He beckoned to a porter, who loaded the suitcases onto a trolley, carried them to the airport door, and placed them on the sidewalk. Isa gave him money for his service, for which the man thanked him profusely. Then he hailed a taxi.

"How long will it take us to our apartment?"

"Traffic permitting, we'll be home in about an hour. You'll love the apartment." Isa smiled tenderly at Aliya.

The drive along the motorway toward the city centre was quiet and almost eerie. Aliya leaned back and looked out the taxi window. It was already close to midnight, and the streets were sparsely populated. Occasionally, the lights of a car passing in the distance flashed. Only through the warm light of the house windows could Aliya glimpse the landscape around her.

After an hour's drive, they finally turned off and drove down a quieter street. The taxi stopped in front of a three-story Art Nouveau house. The house before her had an imposing yet welcoming appearance. It was built of pale stone, with large windows and intricate decorations that reflected the charm of a bygone era.

"Here we are," said the driver, opening the taxi doors. Aliya got out and looked at the building. It was the first time she had seen her new home. Isa took the luggage from the trunk and stepped to her side.

"This is our new home," he said with a smile. "I hope you like it."

"It's beautiful, Isa. Where is our apartment?"

"The middle apartment is ours."

He pointed to the windows in the middle of the three-story house. Except for one window in the attic, the house was plunged in complete darkness and seemed to be in a deep sleep. No wonder at this late hour.

"It's only a ten-minute walk to the hospital. Isn't that fantastic?"

The house was as charming as it was old—with its high ceilings, ornate window frames, and soft, dim light in the entryway. Isa unlocked the massive wooden front door and led Aliya into the stairwell. Unfortunately, the house didn't have an elevator, so Isa took the luggage and carried it up the wide stairs. Aliya followed him. It was a simple but stately staircase made of polished wood. They reached the second floor, and Isa stopped in front of an imposing, heavy door. Her name and Isa's were engraved on the doorbell plate in black capital letters.

"This is our apartment," Isa said quietly. With a solemn look, he pulled the key from his pocket and proudly handed it to Aliya. Hesitantly, she took the key and inserted it into the lock. A soft click sounded as the door opened.

The apartment was beautifully furnished. A wide hallway led to the living room, which overlooked the street. A glass door led to a small balcony with a table and two chairs. A large white sofa formed the centrepiece of the room. In front of it stood a round glass table, on which fresh flowers smiled at Aliya. A brick arch led into another room, the focal point of which was a rustic oak table, around which ten chairs were seated. This room, in turn, was open on one side and led into the kitchen. The bedroom led directly off the living room. It also had a glass door that led to the balcony, which connected the two rooms. After Isa had shown her the bathroom and his study room, he stopped in front of a door. Aliya looked at Isa expectantly.

He opened the door and she looked into a completely empty room.

"This is your kingdom, Aliya. You can decorate the room as you wish," he smiled at her proudly.

Aliya turned on the light, and the room was immediately bathed in a warm, soft light. The walls were painted creamy white, with a soft pink accent where they met the ceiling. A delicate oriental-style lamp hung from the ceiling. Aliya immediately began to mentally plan her room.

"What do you think of your room?" Isa's voice tore her from her thoughts. She turned to Isa, touched his arm lightly, and smiled.

"Thank you. It's beautiful. Now I just want to go to sleep. I'm dead tired."

The next morning, Aliya woke up very early. The room was still in the gentle half-light of dusk, and next to her, Isa slept deeply and peacefully. His breathing was calm and regular. Carefully, Aliya pushed aside the covers and quietly placed her feet on the cold floor, trying not to make any noise.

It was time for morning prayer. The first prayer she would recite here, in her new home in London. She went to her room for it. It was still empty, but for her, it was natural and important to say her first prayer here.

When she was finished, she quietly went into the kitchen. Curious and a little excited, she began opening the cabinets, one by one. To her great joy, she found familiar foods from her homeland—spices, tea, lentils, flour. The familiar scents emanating from the packaging brought a smile to her face.

So that morning, she prepared the first breakfast for herself and her husband. Fresh flatbread, olives, cheese, and sweet honey found their place on the table. Finally, she poured the steaming tea. Its aroma filled the small kitchen.

"Wow, that looks fantastic," said Isa when he came into the kitchen a short time later.

Aliya kept looking at Isa during breakfast. Then she grabbed her heart and asked him: "Isa, why didn't you say your morning prayers this morning?"

Isa smiled briefly.

"We're here in London, Aliya. The strict laws from home don't apply here. Everyone can do whatever they want, including you. You can pray whenever you want, take off your headscarf - do whatever you want."

Aliya winced inwardly. Isa noticed this and quickly added: "But you can also keep everything as you've been doing it. It's up to you."

"I will never neglect my duties. I will follow the Quran, as Allah has commanded me." She looked at Isa with a look that said this topic didn't need to be discussed further.

Aliya felt her heart draw back from Isa a little. She wanted to include him in her next prayer and ask Allah to help him find his way back to Him. She knew he was a kind-hearted man. After all, he was a doctor and helped many people get well every day. Allah would surely forgive him for having distanced himself from him in recent years.

Aliya spent the next few weeks getting to know her new home. When Isa was in the hospital and she didn't have English classes, she took long walks through Paddington, the London neighbourhood where her apartment was located. Praed Street was a wide street lined with large, multi-story buildings and many shops. On one of her many walks, Aliya discovered a small but impressive furniture store on a narrow, cobblestone street not far from her apartment. The shop windows were lovingly decorated, filled with handmade furniture, ornate rugs, and delicate lamps. Above the entrance was a wooden sign with ornate lettering. "Salam" was written on the sign. When Aliya first entered the store, it was as if she had entered another world. It wasn't just the sight of the beautiful traditional furniture of oriental origin, but also the spicy, sweet aroma that filled the entire room. A scent that awakened memories from deep within her childhood and instantly reminded her of her parents' home. She quickly discovered the source of the fragrance. Small metal vessels stood everywhere on the tables, from which smoke spiralled. Incense sticks burned inside, filling the room with an intoxicating scent of sandalwood, myrrh, and rose petals. Aliya closed her eyes for a moment and breathed in her memories deeply.

"The scent is wonderful, isn't it?"

A gentle, friendly voice interrupted her thoughts. Aliya looked up and saw an elderly man whose face was framed by a full, greying beard. His dark eyes rested on her expectantly.

"Yes," Aliya replied. "It reminds me of home."

"Where is your home, if you don't mind me asking?" the man wanted to know, looking at her curiously.

"I'm from Iraq, from Mosul," she revealed freely, without hesitation. Her gaze was always lowered so as not to look the strange man directly in the eye. She hadn't put the niqab back on since flying out of Mosul, but she would maintain her code of conduct even far from home.

"Oh," the man replied, "Mosul is a beautiful city. It was a beautiful city before..." The man didn't continue.

"It's still a beautiful city, sir," she said emphatically. "No matter what happened."

Aliya learned that the man was the owner of the shop and was from Tehran. Her English wasn't excellent, but they were able to communicate well. He told her that he had lived in London for twenty years and was very happy there. After he had shown Aliya around the shop for an hour and told her a lot about the origins of individual pieces of furniture, they arranged to meet the next day. Aliya wanted to come back with Isa to buy some beautiful furniture for her room.

So, little by little, she brought a little bit of home into her home, and after a while, her room was exactly as she had always imagined it.

Not only had she furnished a beautiful room in the last few weeks, but she had also found a fatherly friend in the shop owner. His name was Reza, and both Isa and Aliya liked him very much.

It was Isa who persuaded Aliya to invite Reza and show him the newly furnished room. Reza happily came and brought his wife with him. Amara was a few years younger than Reza. They had met at a wedding reception in London. Their apartment was above the shop. And so, it came about that Aliya frequently stopped there on her walks. First, she went through the shop, looking for something new for the apartment, and then into Amara's apartment and drank tea with her. Amara and Reza regularly came to eat with Isa and Aliya.

On a clear, cool Friday morning, Aliya strolled with leisurely steps toward a grocery store where she planned to buy supplies for dinner that evening. On her way, she repeatedly encountered men in traditional Muslim clothing. The white *qamis* of the older men appeared immaculate, while the younger men often wore colourful versions. Since it was Friday morning and they were all walking in the same direction,

Aliya knew they were heading for Friday prayers. Instead of continuing with her original plan, she spontaneously decided to follow them. Unnoticed, she kept a slight distance and let her gaze wander over the various groups. She was particularly struck by an older man with a silver-grey beard, whose gait, despite his age, possessed a dignified grace. Beside him walked a younger man, perhaps his son, who listened respectfully with his head bowed while the older man spoke.

After ten minutes, Aliya finally reached a street lined with tall chestnut trees. At the end rose a magnificent building that almost took her breath away. The mosque she now stood in front of was breathtakingly beautiful. Its bright walls shimmered in the sunlight, while the ornate minaret towered into the sky. The tiled domes reminded Aliya of shimmering pearls.

She stood in awe and let her gaze wander over the entire mosque. A familiar pounding beat in her heart, for this magnificent building involuntarily reminded her of the great Al-Nuri Mosque in her hometown of

Mosul. She had previously passed by the Al-Nuri Mosque almost every day while shopping. But she had only been allowed inside once. It was the day her older sister, Muna, was to marry her future husband. Her father had only announced the news that morning, the day the wedding ceremony was to take place in the Al-Nuri Mosque, performed by none other than Imam al-Rashid. Aliya still remembered the excitement that had gripped her body that morning. Her heart had probably beat louder than that of her sister, Muna, who had walked through the mosque with graceful serenity.

The Al-Nuri Mosque was beautiful. Its massive arches and intricately carved doors seemed like portals to another world. Aliya could hardly tear her gaze away from the mosque's beauty. As the imam recited the prayers in his powerful voice, Aliya felt almost weightless.

Afterward, there was a small celebration with all relatives and friends in the garden of Muna's husband's family.

The two men had already disappeared into the mosque when the muezzin began calling for Friday prayers. She knew she wasn't allowed to enter the mosque through the same entrance as the men. She slowly walked around the mosque, hoping to find the women's entrance. She spotted it on the right side of the mosque. There was a staircase leading to a pair of wooden doors. Above the door was a sign with the word "women" written in English and Arabic.
"Assalamu alaikum. Are you looking for the entrance to the mosque?"
Aliya turned around in surprise. Standing before her was a woman whose dark eyes sparkled kindly. She wore a simple but elegant headscarf that framed her face and smiled at her. Aliya paused. For a moment, she thought she couldn't believe her eyes. Standing

before her was the woman from the prayer room on the plane to London.

"Yes," she replied, still surprised to see her again.

"I'm new here in town and I followed a group of men hoping they were going to the mosque for Friday prayers."

The woman nodded understandingly. "Come, I'll take you inside."

As they walked up the stairs together, Aliya discreetly studied the woman. It was a pleasant surprise to meet her here, as if fate had decided to cross their paths again.

"My name is Latifa, by the way," she finally introduced herself. "And what's your name?"

"My name is Aliya."

Latifa opened the door, and they both entered the mosque. Behind the large wooden door was a small room with green-speckled floor tiles. There were shoe shelves on the side. Aliya took off her shoes and placed them on the shelf next to Latifa's.

"Behind the right door is a small washroom. You can perform your ablution there. I've done it at home," Latifa pointed to a door labelled "Washroom."

Aliya entered the small washroom, which contained a sink made of antique pink marble and a small, separate toilet. She quickly performed her ablution and returned to the anteroom, where Latifa was waiting for her.

Together they walked through a simple but ornate door into the women's prayer room. Aliya immediately felt the silence that reigned there. A silence that wasn't empty or cold, but filled with a calm, reverent atmosphere. The floor was entirely covered with a large carpet that appeared to be composed of countless small prayer rugs. In warm red tones with gold and blue accents, the pattern ran throughout the entire room.

As they entered, Aliya noticed three other women already in the room. An older woman sat on her heels, her hands resting in her lap, and a younger woman was adjusting her headscarf before moving onto the prayer rug. The third, a middle-aged woman, nodded kindly to Latifa as their eyes met.

That Friday, the imam told the story of a young boy from Riyadh who had immigrated to London with his parents at the age of six. The boy, named Malik, accompanied his father to the mosque every Friday and attended weekly Quran classes. At the age of 18, Malik began reciting Quranic verses in the mosque and shortly thereafter returned to Saudi Arabia, where he could now be heard as a reciter at the al-Haram Mosque in Mecca. A murmur went through the crowd as the imam ended the Friday prayer.

Aliya left the prayer room with Latifa. At the bottom of the stairs, they met the three women from the prayer room. They were standing together, talking and laughing. When they saw Aliya and Latifa, they fell silent. Latifa stopped in front of the small group. "See you later, as always, sisters."

Then she pulled Aliya along.

"Will you come to the mosque again next Friday?"

"Gladly, Latifa."

"Then we'll meet here in front of the entrance, same time as today!"

That evening, as Aliya prepared the meal in her kitchen, she hummed quietly to herself. The scent of spices, cumin, coriander, and cinnamon hung in the air, mingling with the crackling of the hot oil in the pan.

Isa sat at the dining table, his arms folded on the tabletop, watching his wife with a slight smile on her lips. She seemed elated, almost exuberant, as she served the meal.

"You seem so happy tonight," he finally remarked. "Did something happen?"

Aliya placed a steaming bowl of rice on the table, looked at him, and nodded.

"I was at the mosque today."

Isa's eyes lit up. "I'm glad," he said sincerely.

"I met a woman there," Aliya continued, sitting down next to him.

"Her name is Latifa. It's the same woman I met at prayer on the plane."

Isa raised his eyebrows in surprise. "Really? What a coincidence!"

Aliya smiled. "Yes, I could hardly believe it myself. It felt so familiar seeing her again. We hit it off right away."

Isa took a portion of the spicy rice dish, nodded, and then asked, "And will you see her again?"

"Yes, we've arranged to meet next week for Friday prayers."

"I'm glad, Aliya."

"Why don't you come with me, Isa? You have next Friday off."

He leaned back thoughtfully.

"We'll see, maybe I'll actually come. Then you can introduce me to your new friend."

Secret meetings

The week flew by. In the joyful anticipation of seeing Latifa again on Friday at the mosque, everything was particularly easy for Aliya this week. She was in a good mood and had a few lovely evenings with Isa. During these moments, they took time for long conversations to get to know each other better, something they had often neglected. Isa had started his new job at the hospital, which was very demanding for him, and Aliya also had to find her way around the new environment and process the many impressions. But despite all these changes, she desperately wanted to learn more about Isa, about his childhood, his school days, and his family. Isa talked willingly, and he, too, found it fascinating to learn more about Aliya. Their conversations were intense and enriching.

Everything could be perfect, Aliya often thought, but something inside her resisted letting Isa deeper into her heart, and she knew exactly what it was.

In all the weeks they had lived together in London, she had never seen Isa pray. Since their conversation in the kitchen on the first morning after their arrival, she had never brought up the subject again. Isa granted her every wish. She was allowed to go out alone, drink tea with Amara, and visit Reza in his shop. He practically read her every wish from her eyes, but he didn't share her faith, even though he respected it. Aliya didn't like his attitude toward the rules of the Quran, and she noticed how the shadow that had fallen over her heart was becoming darker and darker, and Isa could hardly penetrate it anymore.

The longed-for Friday had finally arrived. But just before they were about to leave, a call came from the hospital. One of Isa's colleagues was ill and he had to step in. So, she would go to Friday prayers alone. If she was honest, she was relieved that Isa wasn't going to Friday prayers with her.

As she stepped out of the house that morning, dark clouds hung heavy over London. They were so deep and black that for a moment Aliya felt as if she could touch them with her fingertips if she stretched far enough. Autumn had the city in its full grip, and the wind tugged at her coat as if it wanted to persuade her to turn back. Aliya pulled her scarf tighter around her neck and set off. The streets glistened with the previous night's rain, and the first autumn storms swept through the alleys. Leaves swirled through the air, and it began to rain. Aliya didn't dare open her umbrella for fear the wind would rip it from her hand. It was the end of October, and the temperatures were already bitterly cold.

Ten minutes later, she arrived at the mosque. From a distance, she could already see Latifa, waiting patiently for her in front of the entrance gate.

When Latifa noticed her, a smile crossed her face and she raised her hand to wave.

"Hello Aliya, good morning! Nice to see you again," she greeted Aliya warmly.

Aliya returned the smile and waved back happily. "Good morning, Latifa! I'm so happy too!"

They entered the mosque together, and Aliya immediately felt a connection. Her gaze wandered through the prayer room, where she saw the three women she had noticed last week, who were friends with Latifa. The women returned her gaze and nodded to both Latifa and Aliya.

Over the next few weeks, Fridays became Aliya's life. Every day, she went shopping, learned English, occasionally stopped by Reza and Amara's house for tea, and once a month, Reza and Amara came for dinner.

Aliya loved cooking food from her homeland for her visitors, and a friendship slowly developed between the two couples. Amara became a motherly friend to Aliya. The highlight of the week, however, was the visit to the mosque with Latifa for Friday prayers.

And so, it was on a cold winter day in December. Aliya woke early to the sound of her neighbours shovelling snow. The scraping noise on the sidewalk echoed at regular intervals through the morning silence all the way up to her apartment. Isa was already up, and she heard the gentle running of the shower from the bathroom. She jumped out of bed and ran to the window, clapping her hands enthusiastically. The city had transformed overnight into a dreamy winter landscape. The snow, illuminated by the streetlights, glittered brightly.

Aliya put on her dressing gown and hurried into the kitchen to prepare breakfast. A delicious aroma of coffee and scrambled eggs filled the room as Isa entered the kitchen.

"Oh, that smells delicious." He smiled at Aliya.

"It's going to be late today. Many colleagues are sick, and I'll have to add half a shift to my current shift. Are you going to the mosque later?"

"Yes, of course, and after that I'll go to Amara and Reza's. They invited me to dinner after I told them last week that you were working until the evening."

"That's nice. See you tonight then."

Isa stood up, kissed Aliya on the forehead, and left the apartment.

After Aliya had cleaned the kitchen, she took a shower and prepared dinner. She didn't know how long she would stay with Reza and Amara. Sometimes she lost track of time because they were so engrossed in conversation. So, she wanted to be prepared so she wouldn't have to rush later.

After completing all the preparations, she put on her thick coat, tied her scarf around her neck, and grabbed her gloves. Then she set off for the mosque. The main street was already well cleared of snow, and even though it was still snowing heavily, the snow melted immediately when it fell on the salted road. Snow piled high along the sidewalks. Aliya walked quickly through the streets, not wanting to keep Latifa waiting. The heavy snowfall made her progress slower than usual, and the side streets weren't plowed.

"Hello, Aliya, wait!"

Aliya turned around and saw Latifa hurrying toward her. Her scarf was askew, and her cheeks were flushed from the cold morning air. She was out of breath, as if she had been running to catch up with her in time.

"Good morning, Latifa." Aliya laughed as Latifa came running toward her like a snowman. Her coat was covered in snow, and a small mound of snow was piled up on her hijab.

Latifa shuddered as she stopped in front of Aliya and laughed too.

"Come on, let's go, then we'll make it in time."

It was nice and warm in the mosque, and during prayer, Aliya felt her tingling fingers slowly thawing again.

Like every Friday, the three women were standing in front of the mosque, chatting, when Aliya and Latifa came out. But this time, instead of walking past the women, Latifa gently pulled Aliya by the arm toward the small group.

"I'd like to introduce you to someone."

The three women raised their eyes curiously and studied Aliya in silence for a moment. They seemed to be exchanging glances, as if they wanted to exchange their thoughts about Aliya.

"This is Aliya," Latifa continued.

"She's only been in London for a few weeks and has now found her way to us."

The women exchanged glances again. Their reserve was palpable, and Aliya noticed that they were approaching her with a certain scepticism.

But then, after a brief moment of hesitation, the oldest of the three women approached and greeted her.

"Welcome, Aliya," she finally said.

Aliya returned the greeting politely and gave her a tentative smile. Latifa took over the conversation and began introducing the women.

"This is Hanna," she said, pointing to the oldest of the three women, whom Aliya had just warmly welcomed. Then she turned to the middle-aged woman. "And this is Farah." Finally, she pointed to the third woman. "And this is Yara."

The three women now smiled warmly at Aliya; their initial reluctance somewhat evaporating.

"I'd like to take Aliya to our meeting this evening," Latifa explained. "You don't mind, do you?"

Latifa asked this as a question, but the way she said it brooked no contradiction.

The women exchanged glances again and then nodded silently.

"See you later then," said Latifa, gently pulling the surprised Aliya away from the small group.

Aliya looked questioningly at her new friend. "What kind of meeting?" she asked, irritated.

Latifa smiled mysteriously.

"We meet every Friday evening, just among women. It's a very informal exchange."

"And what do you talk about?" Aliya wanted to know.

"About our faith," explained Latifa. "We read from the Quran together, share our thoughts and experiences, and talk about anything that concerns us." She paused and looked at Aliya curiously. "I hope you'd like to come?"

"I'd love to come." Aliya was flattered by the invitation.

"Okay, then we'll meet in front of the mosque at six o'clock this evening and then walk together. Is that okay with you?"

"Yes, fine, I'll come."

Before Aliya could reply, Latifa said goodbye with a quick "See you later!" and turned to leave.

Aliya paused briefly, watching her friend hurried down the street in the opposite direction, the one she herself had to take. A light breeze ruffled Latifa's scarf as she disappeared among the passersby.

Aliya remained thoughtful. The evening meeting sounded very interesting, and she was flattered that Latifa had invited her, but she wasn't sure what to expect.

Feeling buoyant, she made her way to Reza's shop. On the way, she stopped at the small greengrocer's on the corner of Praed Street to pick up fresh fruit and vegetables for the upcoming weekend. Reza and Amara would be coming for dinner on Saturday evening. She had bought the meat, a beautiful piece of tender lamb, yesterday. As always, she would bake fresh bread herself.

Towards early afternoon, Isa called from the clinic to tell her he wouldn't be back until late in the evening. Aliya told him about the invitation to meet the women, and he was happy for her.

That evening, Aliya stood punctually in front of the mosque, waiting for Latifa. The wind whistled icy around the corner, and she pulled the collar of her coat up over her chin. The street in front of the mosque was bustling with activity. Many were doing their last-minute shopping and then wanted to hurry home to ring in the weekend. Severe frost was forecast for the night, but the snow was supposed to stop. Aliya pulled her hat even further over her face when she saw someone break away from the crowd of passersby and approach her. It was Latifa.

"Hello Aliya. I'm sorry I'm late. My little son couldn't bear to part with me today," she laughed and took Aliya's arm.

"Come on, let's go, it's not far from here."

Latifa and Aliya walked together through the gloomy, narrow streets of London, whose lanterns made the snow on the cobblestones glitter. They passed the mosque, off the main road. The alleys became narrower and more winding, like a labyrinth, until Latifa finally stopped in front of a small, inconspicuous house.

"So, here it is."

Latifa raised her arm and knocked three times on the old wooden door, and after a short pause, she repeated the procedure as if the knock were a secret sign.

The door opened slowly, and Farah stepped into the dim light. Wordlessly, she took a step to the side to let Latifa and Aliya in.

"Come in," she said quietly, almost in a whisper. Her gaze briefly wandered down the street, first to the right, then to the left, as if she wanted to make sure no one had followed them. Then she closed the door.

"Come," she repeated firmly, her voice a little faintly smiled.

"The others are already here."

Latifa pulled Aliya into a small room at the end of the narrow corridor. Yara and Hanna sat in the middle of the room, bathed in warm light from a small lamp in the corner. Next to them sat two women whose faces were unfamiliar to Aliya. They looked at her curiously.

"This is Eleen," Farah said, looking at the woman sitting next to Yara. Aliya nodded at her.

"Her sister Maha sits next to her. And this is Aliya, she is Latifa's friend, whom I already told you about." The women had made themselves comfortable with soft cushions around a low table. A steaming cup of tea stood in front of each of them. Sweets lay on small, ornately decorated plates—baklava soaked in syrup, dates filled with almonds, delicate pastries with sesame and rose water.

"Take a pillow each and sit with us."

The atmosphere was calm and intimate. Aliya and Latifa each took a pillow from a pile in the corner and sat down with the other women, who had all moved a little closer together. Eleen placed two teacups in front of Latifa and Aliya and filled them with the deliciously fragrant tea.

"Help yourselves," she said, pointing to the plate of sweets. "I baked all of this myself today."

Aliya immediately felt welcome in the group, even though all the women except Latifa were strangers to her. She took a piece of baklava and sipped the hot tea. The women's laughter and the intimate conversations about their families eased her tension, and she, too, spoke openly about herself.

After a while, the mood changed. Hanna opened a book whose golden lettering shimmered in the light—the Quran. In a gentle voice, she began to recite a verse. The other women listened attentively, nodding, letting the words resonate within them. Then a lively discussion began about what they had just heard. Aliya listened, spellbound. Hanna leaned forward slightly, her voice becoming more insistent as she began to place the words from the recited Quranic verse in the context of life in London. She spoke about the coldness in people's gazes, about the emptiness she felt in them, and how different all of this was from what she perceived as true community and faith. The word "unbeliever" was used repeatedly, emphatically. Her words were piercing, full of conviction, almost like an indictment against a society she considered spiritually deranged.

Latifa, who was sitting next to Aliya, stole glances at her, as if trying to gauge her reaction to Hanna's words. But Aliya sat still, her expression calm, almost serene. She said nothing, didn't participate in the discussion, but Latifa noticed the slight gleam in Aliya's eyes, a silent agreement, an inner nod.

Because Hanna's statement corresponded exactly to Aliya's thoughts. These were the very thoughts that had been weighing on her since she learned that she would be moving to London with Isa to live there. In that moment, she felt understood, as if Hanna had finally spoken the words that had been brewing inside her for a long time.

When Aliya went home after this meeting, she seemed calm and relaxed. But inside, she was seething. She felt at home and understood. Finally, there were people around her who thought the same way she did. She was happy to be returning to her apartment. She was looking forward to seeing Isa, but she wouldn't tell him about what was discussed at the meeting. He wouldn't understand because he was like them. His religion wasn't important to him, not anymore. He lived a life like theirs, a life focused on consumption and power, with no time left to devote to prayer and other duties of the Quran.

The meeting had opened her eyes and confirmed what she had known for a long time. She was on the right path. Her beliefs weren't naive or outdated—they were true, consistent, and powerful. She recognized herself in the faces of the others. Their words, their thoughts, their prayers—they were all like an echo and response to what Aliya herself felt. She held fast to her faith, not out of habit, but out of conviction. The Quran was not just a book for her, but a source of truth, a light that guided her through the fog of the Western world.

Isa, on the other hand... he had distanced himself. Not out of malice, not even consciously. The world he had lived in for years had sucked him in, with its noise, its pace, its constant push for more. More work. More money. More success. As a doctor, he did good, no doubt, healing people, saving lives, but nothing weighed more heavily than neglecting one's own religion. Aliya saw this with great concern. He hardly prayed anymore; he no longer spoke about Allah. The Quran was on the shelf in his office, but it remained untouched. She would try to bring him back, with patience but determination, because only then could she save him and open her heart to him again.

As Aliya turned onto Praed Street, she saw light in her apartment. It was coming from the kitchen and radiated a cozy warmth. She quickened her pace and looked at the clock on her cell phone. It was already just after nine. The meeting had lasted longer than she had planned. The others were still staying when she decided to leave. She wanted to be home before Isa and prepare his meal. He was surely exhausted after a day of working double shifts.

She quietly unlocked the apartment's door, hung her wet coat, gloves, and scarf over the heater in the hallway, and went to the kitchen. As she entered, Isa's face lit up.

"Aliya, there you are. You're just at the right time," he pointed to the table, which he had already set and on which the food was already sitting.

"I know you've already eaten, but I thought you'd still be hungry if you were coming home so late."

"I am indeed. I'm sorry I'm so late, but we had a wonderful evening."

"Sit down, I'm really excited to hear what you have to say."

Aliya poured the food onto her and Isa's plates. A delicious aroma hung in the air, while outside a starry, bitterly cold night descended upon the city.

For a moment, only the soft clinking of cutlery could be heard.

"So? How was the meeting?"

Aliya hesitated briefly, then nodded slightly.

"It was... good. Really good. I met some of Latifa's friends, with whom I immediately hit it off. We talked about the Quran and our life here."

Isa chewed slowly, listening attentively.

"That sounds nice. It's good for you, isn't it?"

Aliya smiled gently.

"Yes. It feels like... coming home."

She didn't mention the other side of the meeting. She didn't mention how heated the discussion had become at some points, how harsh words had been spoken about the West and the infidels. Aliya didn't want Isa to know about it—not because she was ashamed, but because she knew he wouldn't understand. Not yet.

Isa leaned back.

"I'm happy for you, really. It's good that you're starting to embrace life here and have made new friends.
I've noticed that it's not easy for you here, and you
miss your family very much."

Dangerous game

In the following weeks, Aliya met regularly with the
women every Friday. The meetings always took place
at the same place, Farah's house. Farah's husband had
been working outside of London for several months.
He worked as an IT specialist for a prestigious company and lived in a small apartment provided by the
company during the workweek. He only stayed in
London on weekends.

It was a Friday in early March, and for the first time in weeks, a hint of spring was in the air. The sun's rays pushed through the thin layer of clouds, tentatively bringing a little warmth to the city.

After the prayer, Aliya and Latifa left the mosque. Aliya took off her thick coat.

"Phew, it's hot," she said, fanning herself with her hand.

Latifa just smiled and also unbuttoned her winter coat. Without a word, they walked a few steps and sat down on a low wall in front of the mosque. Latifa leaned forward a little, placed her hand on Aliya's arm, and spoke softly—almost in a whisper.
"Tonight, we won't meet as usual. There's one small change. We want to meet earlier, at four o'clock in the city, at Piccadilly Circus. We'll distribute verses from

the Quran to the people who are lost. Who are lost. Maybe we can still save some."

Aliya nodded slowly.

"Some might laugh at us or even insult us. But don't let that bother you. If just one of them listens, then that's already a success, and that's enough."

In the afternoon, Aliya stood at Piccadilly Circus. She felt a little lost. There was a hustle and bustle all around her: people hurried past with shopping bags, children laughed as they ran up and down the steps to the fountain, and somewhere a street musician played a melancholy melody on a violin. Her hands clutched a small stack of printed Quran verses, neatly cut out, with a quote on each page. Her gaze repeatedly wandered over the faces passing by. Who among them would listen to her? Who would reject her? What if someone laughed at her? Or worse – shouted angrily at her? Unconsciously, she took a step back, hiding behind a group of tourists who were gesturing loudly toward Piccadilly Circus. Latifa stood a little way away from Aliya. Aliya watched her as she walked unafraid toward people, handing them a piece of paper and saying something to them. Out of the corner of her eye, Latifa must have noticed Aliya's indecision, because she smiled encouragingly at her.

Finally, Aliya gathered the courage and approached a middle-aged woman who was standing at the edge of the sidewalk, rummaging through her bag. Aliya cleared her throat quietly, her voice almost a whisper.

"Excuse me, may I give you a verse from the Quran? It's particularly beautiful."
The woman looked up. Her eyes were bright but tired, framed by fine lines. For a moment, their gaze met, then the woman lowered her gaze, silently shook her head, and turned back to her bag. Aliya withdrew her hand and took a few steps away from her.
Not wanting to be discouraged, she immediately approached the next woman who passed her. She took

the Quranic verse handed to her without comment and moved on. Slowly, the tension left Aliya, and she moved on without fear.

"May I give you a beautiful verse from the Quran?" she asked a friendly, elderly gentleman in a hat who had stopped to watch a pigeon. He smiled in surprise, took the paper, and thanked her with a small nod. A young woman in sportswear smiled politely, shook her head, and said, "No, thank you," and moved on. A young man wearing headphones pulled them out briefly, looked at Aliya, read the words, and then silently put the verse in his jacket pocket.

"May I tell you ...?" she began again, raising her gaze and looking into two eyes she recognized. It was Reza.

"Aliya!" he said, frowning slightly. "What are you doing here?"

Aliya lowered her gaze, feeling a blush rise in her face. She cleared her throat, searching for words.

"I ... I distribute Quranic verses," she said in a low voice.

"Why are you doing this? Does Isa know about this?"

"No," Aliya answered quickly, almost too quickly.

"And he shouldn't know either. It's an event with our women's group from the mosque. Please don't tell him."

She hesitantly held out a piece of paper.

"Would you like one too?"

Reza didn't look at the paper. His gaze remained fixed on Aliya - questioning, examining. Then he slowly shook his head.

"You have to be careful what you do, Aliya. We're not in Iraq. You might end up with the wrong person who won't politely decline."

Aliya nodded slowly, looked briefly at the pieces of paper, then back at Reza. Her eyes hardened.

"Yes, I know. But I still want to do it."

Reza was silent. There was silence between them for a few moments before he put his hands in his pockets.

"Take care, Aliya," he finally said, turned away, and continued walking. Aliya watched him go. She turned around and searched the crowd for the others. She saw Latifa and Farah standing with a man, talking to him. Then the man slapped his hand at the piece of paper Latifa was holding out to him and walked away, cursing loudly. Aliya went to them both.

"Has something happened?" she asked anxiously.

"No, everything is fine. That was just a lost soul, but he will soon feel Allah's wrath." Latifa pursed her lips bitterly.

"Come on, enough for today. Let's find the others and leave."

A week later, Aliya and Isa were invited to dinner at Reza and Amara's house. All day, Aliya had a bad feeling in her stomach, not because of the food or Amara, but because of Reza. Isa noticed her restlessness even before they left the house. "Are you okay?" he asked as he put on his scarf.

Aliya forced a smile.

"Yes, just a little tired."

But in truth, she was tense. Thoughts swirled in her head. What if Reza had talked to Amara about it? What if it came up later that evening that they had met in front of Piccadilly Circus? Reza had clearly not been happy about Aliya distributing Quran verses on the street.

When they rang the doorbell of Amara and Reza's house, Amara opened it with a broad smile. The scent of saffron and roasted vegetables hung in the air, warm and inviting. The house was, as usual, neatly and tastefully decorated, with small lamps in every window niche and scented sticks on the sideboard. Everything radiated harmony, just like their relationship. Only Aliya felt like a disruption to that harmony today.

Reza greeted her warmly, politely, as always - almost too warmly, Aliya thought briefly. Not a word about the afternoon at Piccadilly Circus. Not a questioning look, not a hint. Nothing at all.

Aliya's tension slowly eased.

At dinner, the men talked about football, while Amara asked her about her progress in English class.

It was a thoroughly successful evening, and Aliya, buoyed with relief, linked arms with Isa as they walked home around midnight.

The weeks flew by, almost imperceptibly, and with them, a feeling of quiet contentment grew in Aliya. The small group of women met regularly - sometimes at the train station, sometimes in front of the university, sometimes in the park near the Thames. Their activities were inconspicuous and attracted little attention.

Their Friday evening meetings were quiet, familiar. They often began with tea, with conversations about life, faith, family, and sometimes even worries.

But one evening at Farah's, something was different. It was late summer, and the evenings were getting darker again. The sky was slightly cloudy, and the windows cast long shadows into the living room. Farah had brewed tea with cardamom. The whole house smelled of mint and freshly baked bread. The women sat on cushions and chatted until Latifa took the floor. She was the unspoken leader in the group, sharp in her phrasing, often the one who initiated discussions. On this day, however, her voice was quieter, more controlled, which made it all the more insistent. "Sisters," she began, "what we do is beautiful. It's well-intentioned. But... it's not enough."

The others looked at her. Aliya felt something tighten in her stomach. She knew that tone in Latifa's voice—matter-of-fact, almost cold. And yet there was something new in her tone. Determination. Perhaps even harshness.

"Distributing Quranic verses isn't efficient enough," Latifa continued.

"They hardly read them. Many throw them away before reading a single word, accepting them only out of politeness. Words are no longer enough."

There was a pause. Then, glancing around the room, she said, "There's a new plan. I've thought about it for a long time, and I believe Allah has given me clarity."

The air in the room thickened.

"We will - in the name of Allah - teach them a little lesson."

It was as if a dark veil fell over the group. Some looked down, others nodded barely noticeably. Farah remained motionless, stirring the teaspoon in the cup in her hand.

Only Aliya sat frozen. A lesson? What did Latifa mean by that?

Something inside her wanted to object immediately – but she said nothing, remained calm, and listened as Latifa continued.

"I've received instructions from the very top."

"Who are they at the very top?" asked Yara.

"That's not important," Latifa replied.

"The only thing that matters is that we have the same goal. The unbelievers must be converted or destroyed."

Aliya flinched, but didn't let it show.

"What's the new plan?" Farah was now sitting upright, and her excitement was evident.

"What happens next?" Eleen asked.

The tension between the women was palpable and about to explode. "We'll detonate a small bomb," Latifa said suddenly, with an almost triumphant expression on her face, as if it were the most natural thing in the world.

For a moment, it was as if time froze. The words echoed surreally in Aliya's head. She noticed her heart rate quicken and her grip on the teacup tightly.

"What?" she whispered. Then, more loudly: "No. No, Latifa. We can't do that ... that."

But Latifa was undeterred. Calmly but firmly, she answered: "Aliya, you don't have to be afraid. No one will be hurt. I promise."

But Aliya rose now. Her voice trembled, but it was clear: "Islam is a peaceful religion. The unbelievers must be converted, that's true, but we must not harm people, not even put them in danger. That is not our job, and that must not be our path, Latifa."

Latifa remained calm. She raised her hand in a placating gesture, as if trying to calm the rising excitement. "No one will be hurt. Listen to me. I'll tell you the plan now."

The other women were silent. Some looked down, embarrassed, others looked at Latifa with a mixture of uncertainty and secret excitement.

"Next Sunday," she began, "at the big service at St. Paul's Cathedral. You know how crowded it will be. Hundreds of non-believers will come for Sunday prayers. When everyone is inside, everyone, Aliya, no one outside, a tiny bomb will detonate in the trash can outside the church. No shrapnel. No fire. Just a loud bang. A shock. Nothing more."

She looked around, waiting for the women's agreement.

"The message will be heard. The people will listen—finally. What do you say?"

"Yes, that's good, Latifa," Maha and Eleen were the first to emerge from their state of shock.

"That's exactly what we'll do," the others also agreed.

"Where will we get the bomb?" Hanna wanted to know.

"Don't worry. The bomb will be there on time," Latifa laughed soothingly.

"Who will plant it in front of the church?" Aliya asked, now also slowly coming back to life.

"That's still to be decided. Not by me. The order will come from the very top. They know all of you, know everything about you," she laughed loudly.

As Aliya walked home that evening, her mind raced. Her steps were hurried, mechanical. She paid no attention to the roar of the cars or the babble of voices around her. Not a glance to the right, not a glance to the left. Just straight ahead - as if that way she could escape the noise in her head. The streets of London seemed strange that evening - indifferent. It was windless, but a storm raged within her. Latifa's voice, calm and determined. The other women, how they remained silent - but did not contradict her.

What if Latifa was right? What if what they had done so far really wasn't enough? Again and again, her verses had been rejected. With a smile. With indifference. With open contempt.

The closer she got to the apartment, the more clearly another thought formed. A thought that frightened her and at the same time filled her with a dangerous warmth.

Yes, something whispered inside her. Maybe this is the right way. Maybe this is necessary. Just once. Just so they wake up. So, they no longer overlook us. So, they understand we are here.

The quiet anger that had slumbered within her for so long transformed into something else. Into a dark determination. Otherwise, they don't hear. They don't see us. They throw away the Quran as if it were trash. They despise our words, our lives, our faith.

And suddenly, Latifa's plan no longer seemed like madness - but necessity. Like a last resort. Aliya closed the apartment door behind her. The light in the hallway was dim. From the living room, she heard Isa's quiet voice. He was on the phone with his mother in Mosul, she could tell by the tone of his words.

But inside Aliya, everything was in flux. Something inside her - something that had been foreign to her until recently - was beginning to take root.

She went into the living room and gave Isa a light kiss on the forehead.

"Give your parents my regards."

"My parents are visiting your family. They're having tea together. You can talk to your mother," Isa held out the cell phone to her, and Aliya retreated to her room with it.

The conversation with her mother had done Aliya good. After the phone call, she had snuggled up on the sofa with a blanket. It was already pitch-black outside, and the London summer rain drummed softly against the windowpane, making it even more cozy. She thought of Rais, her little brother, who was probably asleep by now and who, after moving to London, now lived alone with her parents in the house. Her mother had sounded a little sad. She repeatedly complained about the silence that had reigned in the house since Aliya had moved out. She missed her daughters' laughter, the intimate conversations while washing dishes, reading the Quran together, drinking tea in the afternoon, and praying when the whole family gathered in the living room.

Aliya had promised her that she and Isa would come to visit next summer at the latest. She explained that she had found friends with whom she met regularly to read Quranic verses, that she was diligently learning English, and that she was beginning to feel at home in London. Her mother was very happy about this, and her mood brightened again.

Aliya eagerly awaited the next meeting at Farah's. For the first time, she had trouble concentrating on Friday prayers. She kept thinking about the evening meeting. What would Latifa say today, how would things continue?
Evening came, and the women sat in a circle as usual, drinking tea. The only one missing was Latifa. She had already announced the morning after the mosque visit that she would be a little late for today's meeting.

The silence in the room was almost eerie. No one said a word. All that could be heard was the soft crackling of the fire in the fireplace and the sipping as the women carefully sipped their tea. Everyone waited anxiously for Latifa.

Finally, when the tension became almost unbearable, the doorbell rang. Farah slowly stood up and walked down the hallway, each step echoing on the wooden floor.

The women watched her as if their eyes could see through the walls. They hardly dared to breathe, afraid of missing the first sentence Latifa would say to Farah.

An unbearable minute later, Farah and Latifa returned to the living room together.

Latifa sat down with the women, poured herself a cup of tea, and bit into a piece of cake, while six pairs of eyes were fixed on her, waiting for her to speak.

Only when she had put the last piece of cake in her mouth did she raise her head and look around. Then she spoke:

"I'm so late because I had a meeting with someone," said Latifa. Her eyes slid over the women's expectant faces.

"They handed me a package. For the day after tomorrow."
Slowly, she opened her bag and took out a small, tightly tied package - and a cell phone.
"We're supposed to use this to detonate the package."
Again, she let her gaze wander around the group, searching, examining.
"And I've been told who has the honourable task of carrying out this assignment and will place the package in front of St. Paul's Cathedral."

Latifa's gaze slowly wandered around the group. One by one, she looked at the women, deeply and penetratingly, as if she wanted to penetrate their thoughts. Then her gaze settled on Aliya. Unmoving.

"Aliya," she said firmly, "I can announce that you are the chosen one. You have been chosen to place the package - to take on this task that is so important. For us. For our religion.

Aliya flinched; her breath caught in her throat. She should do it. She should take on this task.

She stared at Latifa in disbelief, then turned her gaze around. The women looked at her - open-mouthed, frozen. And then, slowly, one by one, they began to nod.

"Yes, Aliya," Latifa said again, almost imploringly.

"You have been chosen. You will fight for our cause. And I will accompany you."

Slowly, the group began to move. Voices rose, first isolated, then all at once - a jumble of enthusiasm and agreement that made Aliya's head spin.

The women stood up, crowded around her, hugged her, held her hands, and talked to her. Aliya didn't know what was happening to her.

And yet - slowly, very slowly, she felt something change within her. The initial disbelief gave way to a tingling feeling in her chest. Excitement.

It would be her first significant task. For the first time in her life, she was playing a decisive role.

Latifa stood a little way off and watched the scene quietly, almost motionless.

What she hadn't told the others: They had doubts about Aliya. And that was precisely why she had been chosen.

Aliya hadn't been convinced by such actions - too hesitant, too questioning. Now they wanted to see how far she would really go.

This was a test!

If she performed the task well, she would be entrusted with a much greater one. A much, much greater one.

Latifa now took a piece of paper out of her pocket. "Everything is written down here, in detail, the exact schedule for Sunday morning. We'll read the instructions together until we know everything by heart, then we'll destroy the paper!"

A message

Aliya couldn't rest the following night. The steps on the note kept going through her head – she repeated them incessantly so she wouldn't make any mistakes.

The day with Isa had actually been very nice. They had strolled through the city, bought a few little things for the apartment – new curtains, a small plant, even matching pillowcases. In the evening, they had cooked together, laughed, and talked about old stories from Mosul. It should have been light and carefree. But now she lay awake, her eyes fixed on the ceiling. Her thoughts raced in circles, tomorrow's Sunday flickering through her head in countless variations, with small mistakes, with major catastrophes. What if someone was watching her as she discreetly dropped the package into the trash can in front of St. Paul's Cathedral? What if Latifa dialled the cell phone number too early and the bomb exploded in her bag?

Isa breathed calmly and evenly beside her. She closed her eyes and recited a silent prayer, then fell asleep.

When the alarm rang that morning, Aliya mechanically got up and washed for prayer. She had gotten used to the fact that Isa wouldn't get up with her and wouldn't pray with her. Normally, she went back to sleep after prayer, but not today. Isa knew she had an early meeting with the women. She had told him that they were meeting at the mosque today to do crafts with children.

After the morning prayer, she took a shower and dressed leisurely. Afterwards, she cleared away the last traces of the previous evening - empty glasses, a few crumbs from the table, the cushion on the sofa that was still lying askew. Then she made herself a simple breakfast: Arabic bread with some cheese and a small coffee. The kitchen was quiet. No noise from outside, no conversation, no radio.

She sat down at the table, folded the bread neatly onto her plate, took a sip of the still-steaming coffee, and ate in silence. Completely calm. Completely at peace with herself.

Then she set off. She would meet Latifa in front of the mosque and then they would continue on to St. Paul's Cathedral together.

It was cool that morning, and you could tell that summer had finally said goodbye. Latifa was already standing in front of the mosque, and tension was written all over her face, too. They nodded to each other and then continued on together in silence. "Do you have the package with you?" Aliya looked over at Latifa, who had her eyes fixed on the street. She nodded and silently pointed to her bag slung over her right shoulder. After a half-hour's walk, St. Paul's Cathedral suddenly appeared before them - vast, awe-inspiring, as if it had fallen straight from another time into the present. Its mighty dome rose proudly against the sky, shining brightly in the morning light, while the stone columns and arches below seemed to hold every secret of history. The white limestone seemed almost soft in the light. Statues of holy figures stood in niches, silent and watchful, as if watching the two women, and above it all, the cross towered like a silent symbol of the Christian faith. The wind carried the sound of scattered church bells.

"There it is!" Latifa pointed to a bench near the church.

Latifa and Aliya walked over to the bench and sat down. People were now coming from all over, on their way to Sunday services. The church bells were already ringing, the call that told people that the service was about to begin.

"Just like the call of the muezzin," Aliya thought to herself.

When the last ringing had faded, St. Paul's Cathedral lay deserted before them.

Latifa looked at her watch.

"Five minutes," she said to Aliya.

She nodded silently.

Then Aliya stood up. In her hand now was Latifa's bag, which she gripped tightly - so tightly that her fingers turned white. She began to move slowly, her steps purposefully but carefully chosen, toward the wastebasket that stood at the edge of the path in front of the cathedral.

Suddenly, hurried footsteps broke the silence. A young man, apparently late, hurried past her, on his way to the service he apparently didn't want to miss under any circumstances.

Aliya paused, hesitated. Her gaze flickered uncertainly toward Latifa, who was still sitting on the bench, watching her. Latifa nodded calmly, almost imperceptibly.

Aliya stopped, lowered her head as if searching for something in her bag. Her fingers nervously played with the zipper as she waited for the cathedral's heavy doors to close behind the young man. Then she straightened and continued walking - step by step - toward the wastebasket.

She stopped in front of the wastebasket, opened her bag, and pulled out a handkerchief. Then she blew her nose, rummaged in her bag again, and then quickly threw the tissue and the package into the wastebasket. She closed her bag and moved on. Behind her, she heard footsteps approaching rapidly. Her heart suddenly beat a little faster. But if everything went according to plan, they were Latifa's footsteps.

She felt like someone had put their arm tightly around hers. For a moment, she didn't dare look. Then she carefully turned her head.

It was Latifa.

Together they walked a hundred meters further and sat down on another bench, looking toward the cathedral - at a safe distance.

Latifa pulled a cell phone from her bag and handed it to Aliya.

"You finish it," she said firmly.

Aliya hesitantly took the phone and opened it. The number was saved; she just needed to press the green button. She looked down the street again—it was deserted.

"Do it, now," Latifa said, a little harsher now.

One last glance at the street, then Aliya pressed the call button.

A barely visible tremor ran through her fingers, but there was determination in her gaze. She looked at Latifa triumphantly.

Not a minute later, a deafening bang ripped through the silence. The air vibrated. A dull pressure settled over everything, as if the world had held its breath for a moment. Then – dead silence.

They stood up and walked briskly away from the scene. Not a word was spoken. Not a single glance back.

In the distance, the first screams mingled with the growing commotion – first a single one, then several. Fire and police sirens approached inexorably, passing their escape route.

Aliya and Latifa disappeared down a side street, their steps quick but not hasty. They kept up the pace until they were out of sight – home as if nothing had happened.

As Aliya unlocked the front door, she heard a soft splash of water coming from the bathroom. Isa was taking a shower. A brief moment of relief flooded through her, allowing her to catch her breath.

Her hands were still shaking slightly. Not from fear, no – it was the aftereffect of the inner tension she had felt for many minutes and was now slowly beginning to subside.

She went into the kitchen; her gaze fell on the empty table. Isa obviously hadn't had breakfast yet. Almost automatically, she began to brew coffee. She placed Arabic bread on a plate, along with some creamy cheese and fresh salad. When everything was prepared, she sat down at the table. Her thoughts wandered. While she waited for Isa, her gaze slid into the void – calm, but still internally moved by what had happened.

She was proud of herself. She had mastered the task entrusted to her well.

Isa came into the kitchen whistling; he seemed to be in a good mood.

"Hello, my darling. Was the crafting a success?"

"A complete success," Aliya grinned slightly.

Isa turned on the radio and sat down next to her.

"There was an explosion at St. Paul's Cathedral this morning. No one was injured. According to initial findings, the explosive device was in a trash can in front of the cathedral. It is suspected that the perpetrators did not intend to kill or injure anyone. The attack happened shortly after the service began. There were no people in the immediate vicinity at the time. Witnesses are asked to contact the police."

Aliya didn't dare look up. She was afraid Isa could see in her eyes that she might know more about this attack than she was letting on.

"This is really a disgrace!"

Isa slammed his fist on the table.

"What kind of people are these? An attack in front of a place of worship. What would have happened if the bomb had exploded right before the service? Hundreds of people could have been injured."

Aliya had never seen Isa so agitated. The news of the attack had shaken him deeply - he was beside himself with horror. His words were literally tumbling out of his mouth.

"Nothing happened," Aliya tried to reassure him.

"But it could have happened, Aliya - it could have happened."

The next day, Aliya and Isa were invited to dinner at Amara and Reza's. The dominant topic was - how could it be otherwise - the attack. Isa was still agitated. He repeatedly began to talk about everything that could have happened. He repeatedly cursed the "damned terrorists" who carried out attacks in the name of Allah, injuring and killing people.

The news reported that there was still no claim of responsibility and that the investigation hadn't yet uncovered any concrete leads.

"Listen," said Aliya. "We don't yet know who carried out the attack. What makes you think it was an Islamist terrorist attack, Isa?"

"I'm pretty sure of that, Aliya. Just as I'm also sure this was just the beginning." He looked intently into Aliya's eyes. "And next time, it won't just be property damage, but people will be injured and killed. That's how it always starts."

"More tea?" Amara entered the room with a steaming pot of tea, trying to calm everyone's nerves with the distraction.

"Gladly, my dear." Reza took the pot from her and poured the cardamom-scented tea into the cups one after the other, while Amara returned from the kitchen with delicious homemade baklava.

"The police will surely know more soon," he said gently.

Aliya quietly excused herself and went into the bathroom. She needed a few minutes to catch her breath. She leaned against the sink and breathed deeply - and exhaled. As she did so, she looked at her reflection in the mirror. Her skin appeared pale, and her eyes looked dull, having lost the sparkle that always made them shine.

Again and again, she had the impression that Reza was secretly scrutinizing her from the side, as if he wanted to ask an unspoken question:

"Do you have something to do with this? Do you know more than you're saying?"

Then she shook off the thought. How could he know anything? Just because she had peacefully distributed Quranic verses didn't mean she had anything to do with this attack.

Aliya ran cold water over her face, which not only cleared her head but also brought a little colour back to her pale cheeks. After a quick glance in the mirror, she straightened up, collected herself, and finally returned to the others in the living room. She breathed a sigh of relief when she heard Isa talk about his work at the hospital.

What she didn't notice was the gaze Reza was giving her - penetrating and unwavering, as if he wanted to penetrate deep into her innermost being and read her thoughts.

The walk home was quiet and silent. Aliya deliberately avoided speaking to prevent Isa from bringing up the subject again. She took his arm and they quickly walked home; each lost in their own thoughts.

The week passed without any notable events. The next Friday arrived. Aliya couldn't go to Friday prayers at the mosque that morning because she had a doctor's appointment that she unfortunately couldn't reschedule. Instead, she prayed at home.

On Friday evening, she went to her weekly meetings as usual. A subtle, palpable admiration hung in the air. Aliya sensed it clearly. The women were full of respect for what she had done. She had carried out the task smoothly and precisely. Those who had devised the plan were also extremely satisfied. Everything had gone as they had hoped: No one had been injured, and there was no indication whatsoever of who had carried out the attack.

"What happens next?" asked Farah.

"Or do we sit back and do nothing?"

"Everything went according to plan, but have we achieved anything for our cause?" Eleen added.

"You're right, Eleen," Latifa sipped her teacup.

"We haven't achieved anything for our cause yet. But it was a test."

"What kind of test?" asked Aliya.

"A test to see if we are able to implement a plan precisely and without hesitation. No discussion, no questions - simply carrying out the instructions our brothers and sisters have received from Allah." She looked mysteriously into the expectant faces of the women, their eyes glued to her lips.

"There is a new plan our brothers and sisters have devised for us."

A murmur spread through the small living room, after which everyone began to speak at once.

"Quiet, sisters," Latifa raised her hand to silence the women, gaining their full attention.

"This time we will carry out three attacks. They will follow the same pattern as the attack on St. Paul's Cathedral. All three actions will take place simultaneously."

"Who will carry out the attacks?" asked Farah, her eyes full of hope to be part of the operation.

"All of you will be there," Latifa replied.

"Each of you has the honour of acting in the name of Allah."

"And where should we strike?" Farah continued.

"We'll split into groups: Hanna and Maha, Yara and Aliya, Eleen and Farah," she explained, handing each of the women a small piece of paper.

"Here are the plans. Memorize every detail. You'll find out the location, date, time, who will be deployed when and where the day before.

Don't forget – as soon as you've internalized the contents, destroy the papers, just like last time."

The women looked at Latifa and nodded in agreement.

"Let's drink tea together now and not talk about it any further. Instead, let's enjoy the moment of our success and wait calmly until everything begins."

The next few days passed quietly. Aliya prepared intensively for her English exam – it was the important B1 exam she had been working towards for a long time. From morning to night, she immersed herself in her study materials, reviewed vocabulary, refined her grammar, and practiced her pronunciation. She only interrupted her practice to pray and to cook food for herself and Isa.

She often practiced together with Isa, who had almost perfect English. When Wednesday afternoon finally arrived, Aliya felt well prepared. Determined, she set off for the exam.

The exam consisted of a listening comprehension test, free-recounting, and a reading text on which she had to answer questions. Feeling reassured, Aliya finally put down her pen and handed her papers to the examiner with a smile. A heavy burden was lifted from her shoulders, and a sense of relief accompanied her as she left the exam room. Isa was already waiting for her outside the door. He greeted her with a radiant smile and surprised her with the idea of celebrating the successful day together over dinner.

The evening turned out to be wonderful. Aliya felt light, happy, and more carefree than she had in a long time.

In the middle of the night, Aliya was awakened by the quiet beeping of her cell phone. Sleepily, she reached for the device and blinked at the display. A message from Latifa.

"Tomorrow evening, eight o'clock. Everything as agreed," it said simply. Aliya took a deep breath and stared at the few words of the message. Suddenly, her tiredness vanished. She knew what that meant: Now it was starting, there was no turning back. Sleep was out of the question that night.

At exactly eight o'clock the next evening, London was rocked by three massive explosions. The first rang out at Hyde Park Corner, a second followed not far from the British Museum, and the third abruptly shattered the silence outside the university. Thick smoke rose into the sky, sirens wailed, people screamed and ran in all directions.

The locations had been carefully chosen, as they had been the last time - somewhat away from the crowds to avoid injury. But this time the explosions were significantly more powerful, more powerful than the first incident in front of St. Paul's Cathedral. The pressure waves shattered nearby windows, cars honked wildly, and the streets descended into pure chaos within minutes.

When Aliya arrived at the apartment half an hour later, laden with her overflowing shopping bags, Isa was already standing in the doorway, looking at her impatiently.
"Aliya, finally!" he cried with relief.
"What happened? Why are you so excited? I was just shopping."
Isa looked at her in shock.

"Didn't you hear what was going on? There were three explosions! And you didn't come back. I was so worried."

Before Aliya could respond, he forcefully pulled her into the apartment, took her heavy shopping bags, and held her tightly in his arms.

For a moment, she simply remained still, feeling his heartbeat and the relief emanating from him - and only then did she realize what she had just done.

The news came thick and fast that evening. New reports reached the public almost hourly, each one seemingly more dramatic than the last. Reports of the attacks caused unrest throughout the country, not just in London. Around 11 p.m., it was finally announced that there had been injuries. In their panicked flight, people in the crowd had run over each other. An elderly man and a woman had to be taken to the hospital. The man's condition was serious. The police did not say at which of the three locations the man and woman were injured.

Then in the morning, news of a letter claiming responsibility came. What it said and where it was found was to be announced at a press conference around noon.

Isa was on early shift at the hospital, and he and Aliya had only briefly seen each other this morning. He had just gotten up as Aliya was saying her morning prayers in her room. When she came out of her room a short time later, she heard him closing the apartment door behind him. A feeling of relief flooded through her - she was glad she hadn't seen him again. Aliya feared his reaction to the attacks last night. She could still see how upset he had been after the last attack on St. Paul's Cathedral. She was also afraid that he would see clues in her eyes or her behaviour that could betray her. Even though it was unlikely that he would harbour even the slightest suspicion.

She sat on the sofa in the living room all morning. She read the Quran, prayed, and waited anxiously for the announced press conference. What would the letter of confession say? Aliya didn't know herself.

At five minutes to twelve, Aliya turned on the television. She definitely didn't want to miss the eagerly awaited press conference, which was scheduled to begin at twelve o'clock. As soon as she switched on, live reports were broadcast from the scene. A reporter stood in front of the large hall, where a long table had been set up. Behind the table were rows of chairs, many of them with nameplates – including those for representatives from Scotland Yard. The commander and the press officer were also expected.

The atmosphere was tense. The cameras repeatedly focused on the empty table, around which numerous journalists had now gathered. Everyone was eagerly awaiting official information about the attacks.

Shortly after twelve, the moment finally arrived. A group of men entered the room, accompanied by a woman. Without saying a word, they sat down in their designated chairs. The room immediately fell silent.

The press officer was the first to speak. With a serious expression, he described what had happened in brief, matter-of-fact terms. There had been three attacks. Three bombs had exploded simultaneously at different locations in London – at Hyde Park Corner, in front of the British Museum, and in front of the university.

Two people – a 75-year-old man and a 50-year-old woman – were seriously injured. While the woman's health had already stabilized, the man was still fighting for his life. He was hit in the head by an object and is in critical condition and still not out of danger.

The spokesperson then announced that a letter claiming responsibility had been found at the crime scene. He did not specify at which of the three crime scenes the letter had been found. In this letter, the so-called Islamic State claimed responsibility for the attacks. It read verbatim:

"Soldiers of the Islamic State have made a statement. And more will follow."

A murmur went through the hall. The words lingered – threatening, heavy, shocking.

Aliya reached for her cell phone and called Latifa. She was shocked by what had happened; it hadn't been planned that way – a message, not bloodshed. No one was supposed to be hurt. And yet everything had spiralled out of control. Two people are now in the hospital, seriously injured.

"Calm down, Aliya. We've achieved exactly what we wanted. People have been reporting on us since last night – on our group. That's exactly what we wanted to achieve with the attacks."

"But the detonation was much too powerful, how could that have happened?"

"That was exactly what was planned, Aliya." Latifa's voice took on an icy cold undertone.

"The small explosion at St. Paul's Cathedral was just a small prelude and only made a small headline - it wasn't really taken seriously. But now - now we'll be taken seriously. With Allah's help, we've made a statement."

Aliya wanted to protest, but the tone of Latifa's voice brooked no argument.

"Not another word about it, Aliya. Keep a low profile and pull yourself together. We'll meet on Friday as usual." Then she hung up.

New plans

The headlines about the attacks continued. Day after day, they dominated the front pages of newspapers and television news reports. Experts appeared on every evening talk show: terrorism specialists, security experts, Islamic scholars. They analysed, explained, speculated, and provided the agitated audience with seemingly well-founded assessments.

With serious expressions, possible backgrounds were illuminated, perpetrator profiles were created, and political demands were made. Society seemed trapped in a collective state of shock, while the public debate continued to heat up.

Aliya slowly recovered from her shock. Isa watched these talk shows every night and was forthright in his opinion of these terrorists, while a new feeling awoke in Aliya. The more Isa became agitated, the more Aliya's pride grew in what they had done. She had achieved something no one else in her family had ever achieved. People talked about her - they talked about her every day. The people were shocked, helpless, and afraid - afraid of Allah, but with respect for Allah. Latifa was right. They had made a statement - a big statement, and if what Latifa had said was true, then they would make an even bigger statement, and she would be a part of it.

On Thursday morning, the liberating news came over the BBC: Both victims of the attack were out of danger and on the mend. The woman had already left the hospital, and the older man would need some time before he could go home to his wife.
That Friday evening, there was a palpable excitement in the air as the women met. The mood was exuberant, almost euphoric, given the events of the past few days.

Latifa, who had been sitting quietly in a corner, now stepped into the middle of the group with a mysterious smile.

"I have another surprise for you," she said, raising her voice so everyone could hear.

Immediately, a tense silence fell.

"We're having a visitor tonight."

A quiet murmur ran through the room. The women glanced at her curiously and paused.

"What kind of visitor?" Aliya asked curiously.

"Someone who supports our cause, who has planned everything so far, and who will prepare us for the next big step."

No sooner had she said it than the doorbell rang. Farah looked uncertainly at Latifa, who nodded to her to open the door. Farah slowly stood up and walked down the hall to the front door without saying a word. The others heard her speaking quietly to someone - muffled voices, difficult to understand. A moment later, she returned. A man entered the room behind her.

Aliya held her breath. It was the man she had seen with Latifa at the airport. It was definitely him. She still remembered the moment they retrieved their luggage from the conveyor belt. Aliya had assumed it was Latifa's husband, because they had also sat next to each other on the plane from Mosul to London. Why was he here now?

The man was tall, wearing a long coat. His long beard was thick and well-groomed, with a shaved mustache - a detail that immediately caught Aliya's eye and suggested his deep-rooted religious convictions. He entered the room slowly. The women's conversations died down. His gaze wandered around the room - calm, examining, until it finally settled on Latifa. For a moment, they looked at each other, as if silently communicating. Latifa returned his gaze. She seemed composed, but for a moment, an expression flashed on her face that Aliya couldn't identify, a mixture of tension and familiarity.

Latifa stood up and approached the man.

"May I introduce you? This is Abu Khalid."

The man nodded briefly around the group and avoided looking directly at the women.

"Abu Khalid has great plans for us, dear sisters. The signs we have made, which have brought great attention to our cause, have been viewed with favour." Latifa's eyes flashed as she spoke.

"But now Abu Khalid will explain everything else to you." She returned to her seat.

Abu Khalid slowly scanned the room. His face held a look of deep determination. A tense silence fell over the women - so quiet that Aliya could hear her own heart beating.

Slowly, almost deliberately, Abu Khalid began to move. Step by step, he crossed the room, as if to reinforce the meaning of his words with each step. No one dared to move, for fear of disturbing the tension with a mere sound.

Then he stopped. He turned - his gaze was calm but penetrating - and looked at each of them. "Three of you," he began slowly, "will receive a great honour. You will sacrifice yourselves - as martyrs - in the name of Allah. Your death will not be the end, but entry into eternal paradise. An act that requires courage, absolute devotion to your Lord, and true strength."

A whisper ran through the room, but no one dared to speak out loud.

"You will decide which of you will take on this task," Abu Khalid continued.

"There will be no order, no coercion, only your conviction."

Latifa stood next to the door, silent, waiting. Abu Khalid pointed to her.

"Latifa will accompany and support you. She herself will not be part of this mission. Her task will be to maintain the connection between you and me."

He remained silent, as if to emphasize his words and give the women time to process what they had heard.

"But don't forget one thing," he said with a serious expression, "you are all chosen. Whether you fight, suffer, or sacrifice yourselves, you are serving a great cause. And for that, paradise will be open to you."

The women looked at each other. Aliya could see admiration in their eyes, but also doubt and fear. Abu Khalid continued:

"The plans for this great task have already been written, and its execution will grant you the highest level in paradise a woman can achieve."

Aliya looked at Latifa, who was hanging on Abu Khalid's every word, her gaze leaving no doubt that she admired him for everything he said and did. He then turned to Latifa and took a step toward her.

"Latifa, in a week I would like to have the names of the women who have chosen to give their lives for Allah and ascend to eternal life."

Then he turned to the women again.

"In a week, I will visit you again and inform you of the plans. I expect each of you to be ready to give your all and to choose carefully which of you will have the honour of entering eternal life soon."

As suddenly as he had appeared, Abu Khalid disappeared again. Not a single word wasted, not a gesture wasted, just a final glance around the group of women. For a moment, there was something unfathomable in his eyes: determination, anticipation, perhaps also the cold echo of what he left behind. Then a brief, barely perceptible nod, and he was gone.

The door closed.

What remained was an oppressive silence. The women sat motionless. As if someone had stopped time. No one spoke. Their faces were blank, their eyes staring into nothingness.

"More tea?"

Latifa finally broke the silence and served the women hot tea one by one.

"I think a little sweet tea will do us all good right now."

"I'll do it!"

The words came suddenly, almost like a cry, yet sounded clear, determined, final. All heads turned at once. Eyes turned to Hanna.

"Yes," she repeated, a little quieter now, but no less determined.

"I'm ready. I'll sacrifice myself," she said. "For our cause."

No one spoke. No one contradicted her. The faces of the others reflected surprise, admiration, and perhaps even a little relief.

Latifa was the first to find her voice.

"That's great, Hanna," her voice trembled as she said the following words to Hanna:

"I'm incredibly proud of you."

Then she stood up, walked to the large bookshelf, and pulled out the Quran. She opened it solemnly, leafed through it, and read aloud:

"Surah Al Imran, verse 169. Do not think that those who die for Allah are dead. Rather, they are with their Lord and cared for by Him."

She slowly closed the Quran and looked up triumphantly. Her hand rested on Hanna's arm.

"I will tell Abu Khalid about your decision today."

"I want to do it too!" Yara straightened. Her voice was calm and firm, and a light began to shine in her dark eyes.

Latifa turned around, her lips curling into a warm smile.

"Yara, how beautiful."

She reached for Yara's hand and held it for a moment, as if to give her strength.

"Now all we need is a woman," she said in a calm voice, "one who is willing to give everything for our cause and for Allah."

Her gaze wandered to the other women, to Farah, Aliya, Eleen, and Maha. Aliya held their gaze. She saw the others lower their heads, as if afraid that Latifa could see their fears in their eyes.

"Aliya, you've proven yourself twice already and been strong. That's why my words are directed at you - Farah, Eleen, Maha. I want to give you the chance to be part of it first. Part of something bigger. It's a decision that requires courage - I know that."

The room remained silent. None of the women moved. Instead, they looked at the floor, as if their gaze might find an answer there. Each of them secretly hoped the other would speak up first.

Latifa took a deep breath. Her words became gentler now, almost comforting. "If you're not ready yet - if your hearts aren't ready yet - then take your time. There's no need to rush into anything. You still have until next Friday to decide. You, Aliya, can decide too."

She paused briefly and glanced around again.

"I'll speak to Abu Khalid this evening. I'll tell him that you, Yara, and Hanna have chosen our path."

Isa had taken the entire week off. So, he spent the whole day at home, strolling around the apartment, tinkering here and there, or simply sitting in the living room and reading.

For Aliya, his constant presence was a welcome distraction - at least in part. Her thoughts constantly revolved around the new plan. A plan that hadn't yet been spoken. But above all, the third person Abu Khalid needed to carry out his plan was missing. Again and again, Aliya reached for her phone, unlocking it almost automatically, only to stare at the WhatsApp group again. There was no new icon, no message, and with every passing minute, with every passing day, the uneasy feeling that time was running out grew within her.

Isa noticed that Aliya repeatedly looked at her phone. "Is everything okay, Aliya?"

"What, yes, why?" Aliya answered absently.

"Well, because you're always staring at your phone."

"Oh, I'm waiting for a message from the language school group about the exam results."

Isa was satisfied with her explanation, and Aliya was glad he didn't ask any more questions.

On Monday, Isa and Aliya decided to go into town. Isa had decided to buy new shoes. They walked into town - a trip that took about an hour. Isa had insisted. "A little exercise and fresh air will do us good," he had said, and Aliya had just nodded.

Halfway there, they passed Reza's shop. Reza was standing in front of his shop, examining the window, which he had newly decorated. When he saw them, he raised his hand and waved to them. Aliya and Isa stopped. A brief, cordial exchange ensued - how things were going, how the shop was doing, and whether they wanted to meet for dinner again some- time. Reza nodded enthusiastically, but his eyes kept wandering to Aliya. Not intrusively, not unpleasantly - but noticeably. His gaze kept trying to catch her eye.

Aliya ignored his gaze and avoided him - still worried that he might start talking about their meeting at Piccadilly Circus.

Finally, they arranged to meet for dinner at Amara and Reza's the following Saturday evening.

"Amara will cook us an Iranian specialty. You'll be in for a treat," he said with a twinkle in his eye.

Aliya and Isa spent a lovely day in the city. The streets were bustling but not crowded, and a gentle spring breeze made strolling through London's streets pleasant. For a few hours, everything else was forgotten - the plan, the uncertainty, and even the uneasy feeling of her being the third person.

Aliya felt light. She laughed a lot with Isa and even let herself hold his hand in public. She was happy.

Isa finally found a pair of sneakers in a small shop on Portobello Road. It was a shop with old-fashioned wooden floors and a saleswoman who explained each model with passion, as if the fate of the world depended on it. The shoes fit perfectly.

"They're for jogging," Isa said proudly, because he had decided to start exercising. He even tried to persuade Aliya to buy a pair and go jogging with him. But Aliya indignantly rejected this suggestion. They stopped for lunch at a small Italian restaurant diagonally across from Piccadilly Circus. After dinner, they walked for another hour through Hyde Park. The sun was shining and already full of energy. As the afternoon slowly turned into early evening, the two set off back home. Aliya's feet ached from all the walking, so they took the subway back home.

That evening, as Aliya stood in front of the mirror brushing her teeth, the thoughts suddenly returned. Her face darkened. How could she have let herself go like that? She had even skipped the midday prayer because there was no way to perform it. She had walked through the city hand in hand with her husband like a lovesick teenager.

"Oh Allah, forgive me for my sins." She dressed for the night and quietly went to her room. Darkness had already fallen over the city, and only the dim light from the street lamps fell through the window. Aliya drew the curtains. No one should see her. She unrolled the prayer rug, carefully aligned it toward Mecca, and stood with her hands by her ears, her forehead still.

First, she performed the midday prayer, then she performed the delayed evening prayer. And then she sat there in silence for a long time. Her hands open in her lap, her gaze lowered. Her lips moved softly, almost in a whisper, as she recited dozens of duas. She spoke as if she needed to pray for freedom from the beautiful day she had spent with Isa.

Afterward, she went to bed without going back to Isa. From the living room, she heard his voice whispering – he was on the phone with his mother in Mosul.

The next Friday came, and with it the next fateful meeting. The sky was heavy with leaden clouds, reflecting Aliya's inner turmoil. On the way to Yara, a plan matured in Aliya. A plan that would finally free her from the guilt of that day, when she had indulged in many superfluous things and behaved in public like a kafir, an unbeliever. And now she would make amends. She would be the third; she would sacrifice herself for Allah with Hanna and Yara. As soon as she finished the thought, a strange calm flooded through her. Not cold, not fear - but something relentless and pure.

Without hesitation or pausing, Aliya continued on to Farah's house. Arriving there, she knocked vigorously on the door. Surprisingly, Latifa opened the door.

"Hello Aliya, I'm so glad you're here! There's good news!"

"What news?" Aliya asked curiously.

"Come in first - the others are already waiting."

Aliya took off her coat, hung it neatly on the coat rack, and carefully placed her shoes underneath. Then she followed Latifa through the hallway into the living room, which, as always, smelled of a mixture of hot tea, pastries, and scented sticks. In the living room, the others were already sitting in a circle on the floor, excited and full of anticipation for what would happen next.

Aliya sat down in the empty seat next to Maha and Eleen - she could hardly wait to tell the others that she had decided to be the third member of the group. "It's good that we're all here," said Latifa, making a mysterious face.

"So, I can tell you the news now, before Abu Khalid joins us," Latifa said firmly. Aliya felt a sense of unease spreading within her. Her thoughts raced, but she remained silent.

Latifa glanced briefly at Maha, who sat there with a withdrawn expression.

"Maha has been deeply introspective over the past few days," Latifa began, "and yesterday she told me that she, too, is ready to sacrifice herself for our cause."

A moment of silence hung in the air - then it broke like a dam, and the women all spoke at once. Each expressed their appreciation and pride to Maha. Only Aliya remained silent. She sat frozen, her gaze fixed on the floor.

"Aliya?" Latifa asked, astonished. "Are you all right? Aren't you happy for your sister that she's chosen Allah?"

Aliya slowly raised her head, her eyes sparkling with determination.

"I've made my decision too," she said calmly but firmly.

"I want to be the third in the alliance."

For a moment, there was a deep silence in the room. Then all eyes turned to Aliya.

"Aliya, that's wonderful. I always knew you were a brave woman," Latifa looked at Aliya in admiration.

"But what do we do now?" Eleen said, looking at her sister Maha, whose eyes had taken on a worried expression.

"We're waiting for Abu Khalid. He'll decide which of you two it will be," Latifa looked at the clock on the wall.

"He'll arrive here in an hour. Until then, I don't want us to talk about it any further. He'll know what the right decision is."

It was the quietest hour the women had ever spent together. A strange heaviness hung in the air. They drank their tea and bit into their pastries in silence, but no one spoke a word. Each was lost in her own thoughts, moved by the decision the four of them had made and by what lay ahead.

Then, finally, the liberating ring at the doorbell. A brief sigh of relief went through the group. Abu Khalid had arrived. His gaze swept around the group, examining them. The atmosphere changed instantly - the time of silence was over.

With a brief, respectful nod, he greeted the women before turning his gaze to Latifa.

"And how are things, sister?"

His voice was deep and firm.

"Have you all made a decision who the third person will be?"

Latifa slowly rose.

"Yes," she answered. "More than that, two more women have even been found - Aliya and Maha."

She let her words sink in for a moment, then added, "I trust that you will make the right decision as to which of them is best suited to our plan, Abu."

Abu Khalid silently let his gaze wander from Aliya to Maha. His eyes were calm, searching, as if he wanted to peer deeper into their souls than words ever could. Then he fell silent. Minutes passed in tense silence, in which no one dared to move. Then his gaze fell on Aliya.

"Aliya, you have already shown twice how important our fight against disbelief in the world is to you. You have carried out everything exactly according to Allah's will, without asking questions, without hesitation. You deserve a reward. That is why I chose you."

Aliya held her breath. She could hardly believe it: she was chosen. She would be allowed to be there.

"Thank you, Abu Khalid," she said quietly. "Thank you for having so much faith in me."

Abu Khalid nodded at her seriously.

"Inshallah, you will master this task too," he said calmly.

Then he turned to Maha. She sat quietly, her gaze fixed on the floor, her hands tightly clasped in her lap.

"Maha, don't be sad. Allah will find an honourable task for you too."

His gaze fixed on hers.

"You will undoubtedly play a significant role in our plan, just like all of you. Each of you will be a part of it, one way or another."

A silent agreement settled over the group. The decision had been made, and there was no turning back.

Abu Khalid took a step back, his gaze sweeping around the group one last time. Then he sat down a little way off on a small cushion at the edge of the room. His posture was upright, his demeanour calm, but imbued with authority.

"I will now explain the plan to you. Each of you will be informed. But I ask, no, I demand - absolute secrecy."

He deliberately let the words fall slowly so that their meaning could sink in in the women's minds.

"Not a word. To anyone. Not to your families, not to your friends, and not to each other. What I'm about to tell you will stay in your hearts and minds. Anything else jeopardizes our cause."

The women nodded, some seriously, others nervously.

"Everything is planned down to the smallest detail - the place, the day, the time, when the attack will take place. The only thing I'm going to reveal to you today," he said, looking each woman in the eye again, "is the task each will take on."

"And when will we find out when the day is and where everything will take place?" Maha asked.

"When the time comes." Abu Khalid stood up and walked slowly across the room. He stopped at the window and looked into the darkness, as if checking that no one was watching the house from the garden. Then he drew the curtains noisily. "It could be tomorrow, next week, in a month, or even a year from now." He turned back to the women and returned to his seat. Latifa stared at him in awe, hanging on his every word as if trying to draw the words out of them with her eyes.

"Yara, Aliya, and Hanna, you are the key players in our plan. Our greatest hope and deepest trust rest on you. You will sacrifice yourselves - for Allah, for our cause, for what we believe in. Your names will not be forgotten. Your deeds will shine like a star in the dark night. I promise you that."

He paused briefly, as if acknowledging the moment, then continued.

"You will ascend to the highest level of paradise. A level that few women reach. Your sacrifice will pave the way for you, a path that only the chosen ones walk."

"What will our task be?" Aliya interrupted him impetuously.

"All right, sister. I understand your excitement. But be patient."

"Sorry, Abu Khalid. I didn't mean to be rude. Please forgive me."

"You, Hanna, and Yara will become great martyrs. You will be given an explosive belt. The detonator will be activated from outside. Just like in the last attacks. The operation is completely safe, and the explosives will not be detected under your abayas."

"And what about us?" Maha looked at Abu Khalid.

"You, Farah, and Eleen will each accompany one of the three and stand by her until the last minute. You will all be in the same place, positioned so that our operation will attract the greatest possible attention. It will be an inferno."

A smile flitted across Abu Khalid's face.

"Latifa will be the mediator between us. From her, you will learn the location and your respective positions, as well as the exact schedule. You won't find out the day and time until hours before it starts."

A palpable commotion arose among the women – but it wasn't tense, but rather joyful, expectant commotion. Voices rose, everyone was talking at once, laughing quietly, some whispering excitedly. In the midst of this lively hubbub, Latifa and Abu Khalid met each other's eyes. For a moment, time seemed to stand still. They nodded to each other wordlessly, a silent agreement. Then Abu Khalid turned away and silently disappeared from the room. Latifa let the women have their say for a moment, giving them space to express their emotions. Finally, she clapped her hands vigorously several times. There was silence. With a calm gesture, she opened the Quran in front of her, turned to a page, and began to recite a few verses in a firm and clear voice.

That day, Aliya returned home with great anticipation. The feeling of being part of something great, of playing an important role in it, made her proud, and she felt closer to Allah than ever. Hopefully, she could hide her feelings from Isa; he mustn't notice anything, and who knows how long it would be before they would strike. Latifa concluded by saying, "You are sleepers now, and I will awaken you when the time is right..."

Afterward, she hugged each of them and wished them strength.

The attack

The following weeks passed quietly and uneventfully. As usual, Aliya went to the mosque every Friday, and in the evenings, she met with the women. It was a steady rhythm, a calm beat in which she moved – almost as if in a fog, out of habit and tense anticipation. But not a single word was said about what was to come. This was Abu Khalid's order, and they all adhered strictly to it – out of caution, out of loyalty, out of conviction. No one wanted to risk jeopardizing the planned action.

Once a week, Aliya spoke to her mother on the phone. It was a brief ray of hope amidst the silence. Her mother talked a lot – about everyday things, about the home Aliya had left behind. She told them how beautiful the garden had become that summer, how big the small date palm Aliya had planted had already become, how it now reached above her head. And again, and again she emphasized how much they missed Aliya. Aliya's heart clenched. The thought of never seeing her parents, the familiar garden, her date palm again hung like a dark shadow over her thoughts.

At the end of the conversation, her mother had extracted a promise from her that after the summer, she and Isa would come to Mosul for three weeks to visit the family.

It was a warm Saturday morning when Aliya decided to go to the market to buy fresh fruit and vegetables for the weekend. As she passed the mailbox in the hallway, she paused for a moment and opened it. There was an envelope inside, plain and official. The sender was the language school. She had already forgotten about it. Heart pounding, she took the letter and hurried up the stairs back to the apartment. Isa was sitting at the kitchen table reading the newspaper.

"The letter arrived," Aliya said breathlessly.

"From school—about the exam results."

"So? What does it say? Did you pass?" Isa asked curiously.

Aliya shook her head.

"I don't know. I haven't opened it yet."

"Then open it." Isa laughed.

With trembling fingers, Aliya tore open the envelope. Her eyes scanned the lines, searching for the crucial sentence. And then - very slowly - a smile spread across her face.

"I did it," she whispered. "I passed the exam."

She was still holding the paper in her hand as if it were something precious. There it was, black on white: the English certificate that opened the door for her. She could now go to work if she wanted, earn her own money. Isa approached her and hugged her.

"Congratulations. I'm very happy for you."

"Thank you, I'm happy too."

Then she slowly turned around. Isa shouldn't have seen how her eyes grew sad and darkened. A shadow had fallen over her face, quietly, almost unnoticed, but inexorably. She thought of her task, of what lay ahead of her and from which she shouldn't allow herself to be distracted. At that moment, passing the exam no longer seemed like an achievement, but something insignificant, almost meaningless - a beautiful but useless piece of paper in a world where entirely different things mattered.

"I'm going to the market now," she called to Isa. She took the exam certificate to her room and placed it neatly folded in the drawer of her small dresser, where she kept many a secret. Then she set off for the market and remembered the important things in life, and that didn't include passing the exam, with the prospect of a job and a Western life with Isa in London. Summer passed, the leaves turned yellow and red and blew through the streets of London with the first autumn winds. Aliya had taken her coat out of the closet because it was already getting bitterly cold in the evenings. Thoughts of the plan were slowly fading. It had been several months since Abu Khalid had come to their meeting and revealed the first details of the plan.

The trip to Mosul, which Aliya had promised her mother, had to be postponed because Isa couldn't get time off. There had been a vacancy at the hospital for months. Until no one was found, he couldn't get leave. But they planned to make up for the trip in the spring. Aliya was fine with that. She didn't want to see her family now, and she couldn't leave London anyway. What if it had suddenly started and she had been in Mosul? That way, she didn't have to come up with an excuse.

The following Friday, Latifa didn't show up for Friday prayers at the mosque. She hadn't told anyone why she hadn't come.

Aliya knelt on her prayer rug in the mosque. The room was silent, filled only by the soft murmur of the women praying. But Aliya's mind wasn't entirely on the words. She repeatedly raised her eyes to the door each time it opened, hoping Latifa would come in. But Latifa didn't come.

With each minute, her unease grew. The other women also began to look around, whispering questions to each other. It was unusual that Latifa hadn't shown up for prayer. She, who was usually the first to arrive. Even during the women's weekly evening meeting, her seat remained empty. They waited, full of anticipation, with growing concern. But Latifa didn't appear. The women had just decided to end the meeting a little earlier that evening when the bell rang. Yara rose, crossed the hall, and opened the door. Voices drifted quietly into the room – muffled, barely audible. When she returned, she wasn't alone. Latifa entered the room at her side, followed by Abu Khalid.

It's starting – Aliya immediately thought. This could be the only reason Abu Khalid was here today, coming to the meeting with Latifa. Without further ado, he began to speak: "Sisters, the time has come. Are you ready to follow the path Allah has shown us?"

Aliya heard a slight tension in his voice that she didn't recognize, as he usually seemed strong and confident. The women nodded expectantly.

Abu Khalid went to the table directly by the window and drew the curtains. From the bag he wore over his shoulder, he pulled some notes out, placed them on the table, and arranged them in six neat piles in front of him. Then he beckoned the women over to him –

one after the other. Each stepped forward quietly and handed each one of the six carefully prepared stacks. The ritual was performed wordlessly. When the last woman had taken her place again, he looked up.

"In your hands you hold the detailed plan of our mission. Each of you now has one hour to memorize everything very thoroughly. After that, everything will be destroyed in the fireplace. Latifa and I," he looked at Latifa, who was watching everything from the doorway, "will not let you out of our sight. No piece of paper may disappear into your pockets. You must memorize every detail. No piece of paper leaves this room. You must store everything," he looked intently at the women, "and I mean everything, every word, every place, every minute of the plan in your heads. Do you understand that?"

The women nodded silently and immediately began their task.

Aliya found it very difficult to concentrate. Again and again, she lowered her gaze, letting her eyes wander furtively to the others. Abu Khalid and Latifa stood there frozen, their gazes fixed on the women. The letters on the page in front of her blurred, dancing before her eyes, and she had to squint again and again to be able to continue reading. She felt Hanna's gaze – searching, and when she looked up, she saw the fear in her eyes. Aliya tried to radiate calm, to reassure her with a look. But she realized it wasn't working. Hanna turned away, unsettled. After Aliya read the text a third time, she was certain. She had internalized every detail of the plan. Deeply enough that tomorrow, when the time came, she would remember everything. Because tomorrow was the day, they had all been waiting for so many weeks.

"Farah," Latifa's voice broke the silence.
"You can light the fireplace now."
Farah stood up, walked over to the fireplace, and lit the fire. One by one, the women approached the blazing flames and threw in their notes.

"We'll meet here tomorrow morning at 9:00. We'll leave at 9:15. We'll all go together. Do you understand?"

The women nodded and went home immediately. Latifa stayed behind with Abu Khalid and Farah.

"I have to get a few things. See you tomorrow," Aliya said, waving goodbye to the others. Then she turned away and disappeared down a narrow side street. She wanted to be alone - to spend the walk back in silence, not to have any conversations. As she turned onto Praed Street, she saw Isa standing at the window. She knew she was late, and she also knew Isa would be worried.

She had already bought some things at the market that morning, giving her an excuse for being so late.

Aliya cooked a lavish dinner for Isa and herself as compensation. It felt like a last meal - and in a way, it was, at least for Aliya. A faint smile crossed her lips.

It wasn't mirth, but a quiet irony that briefly made room for itself.

The night was very restless. Aliya couldn't sleep. Only when dawn broke did she fall into a light sleep, interrupted only shortly after by the ringing of the alarm clock. Isa had left for work early that morning, so Aliya could prepare for the big day in peace. She took her time for a long shower, letting the warm water run over her body for a long time. Afterward, she made herself a strong cup of coffee. She didn't feel hungry. When she was finished, she made her way to Farah's, not wanting to be late at all. The streets seemed almost empty, and she only encountered a few people – it was Sunday, and many were taking advantage of the day off to sleep in. It was already quite chilly this morning, and Aliya pulled her coat tightly around her, keeping it closed at the collar to prevent the wind from getting inside. She had deliberately put on her long, loose coat so no one could see what she was wearing.

From a distance, she saw Farah already standing at her front door, waiting. When she saw Aliya approaching, a smile of relief crossed her face.

"Hello Aliya," she whispered, as if afraid of betraying her plans if she spoke loudly. Farah had large shadows under her eyes, as if she hadn't slept all night. Aliya stood beside her, and together they waited for the others, silent, each lost in her own thoughts.

Little by little, the women arrived. At exactly nine o'clock, a minibus slowly turned the corner and stopped directly in front of the women. At the wheel sat a man Aliya had never seen before. Next to him, in the passenger seat, she recognized Abu Khalid. The strange driver wore a black turban wrapped tightly around his head. His gaze was fixed impassively, almost as if he wanted to be distracted by nothing and no one—silent, serious, as if carved from stone. With a quiet hiss, the sliding side door of the vehicle slid open. Inside sat Latifa, who nodded to the women with an inviting gesture and signalled them to get in. The women boarded the bus one by one. It was large enough for each to sit comfortably. Then the driver started the car and drove off. According to the plan, they would reach their destination - the site of the planned attack - in an hour and a half. After half an hour, they left the motorway, drove for ten minutes on a country road, and then turned onto a track that led to a small but densely wooded area. Another five minutes later, the driver stopped the car.

Abu Khalid opened the front door and got out. No one dared to say a word. He went to the trunk, took out a large suitcase, and placed it in front of the bus. Then he gave a quick nod to the driver, who also got out and opened the side door so the women could all get out.

"This is Omar," Abu Khalid pointed to the driver.

"He will now put the explosive belt on you. Follow his instructions exactly."

Aliya watched as Omar took the first explosive belt from the suitcase. He walked over to Hanna. She opened her coat and took it off. Omar took the belt and put it on Hanna. With a loud click, the buckle clicked into place. Omar looked up, met Hanna's eyes, then turned to the women.

"There's no way for you to open the belt now." He pulled a small device from his pocket that resembled a lighter.

"And now," he pressed a button on the top of the device, "the belt is armed." He pointed to a small, flashing red light on the side of the belt.

"That's the signal that the belt is activated. There's no turning back now."

Aliya flinched and glanced quickly at Hanna, who stood motionless - as if she had suddenly fallen out of the world. Her face was rigid and unmoving, but her eyes betrayed confusion. It seemed as if she hadn't

understood what Omar had just said. That one inconspicuous sentence, that the belt wouldn't open later,
was a tiny but crucial detail that wasn't on the notes
they had memorized with such precision and disci-
pline.

Omar then took the second belt from the suitcase and
approached Aliya. Aliya let the belt be tied on her as
if in a trance, a slight panic rising within her as it
clicked into place. She had submerged herself mentally to avoid screaming out loud. Images of her life
flashed before her. She saw her mother waving to her
as she walked hand in hand with her friend into
school - her first day of school. Aliya was very proud
at the time and full of curiosity. Inevitably, images of
the day came to mind: there was a knock on the class-
room door and two heavily armed Islamic militants
stormed into the room, ordering the teacher to send
the girls home immediately and forbidding them, under penalty of law, to return to school the next day.

When she came to, the bus was already driving along the motorway. The engine hummed steadily; the asphalt passed by in grey streaks beneath them. Aliya couldn't remember how she had gotten on or even how they had gotten back onto the road. Everything was as if erased - a black hole in her memory. Apparently, her subconscious had taken control and put her into a state of complete isolation to protect her from reality. An internal mechanism that kept her calm even though everything inside her wanted to scream. But was it really just the mind that had shielded her? No. In her heart, she was certain: It was Allah who had carried her through this grotesque situation - with an invisible hand, quietly but powerfully.

"We'll be there in a quarter of an hour. Get ready, sisters," Latifa broke the silence, her voice euphoric.

Aliya saw Yara and Hanna sitting motionless on the bench opposite her. They were now driving off Motorway 24 and a few minutes later stopped at a sprawling intersection. Two green road signs, shaped like arrows, rose high in the air. Each sign depicted a small, white airplane. One path led to Gateway, the other to Heathrow. The car switched on its indicator and turned toward Heathrow. The destination was clear.

A few minutes later, the next sign appeared: Heathrow – 2 miles. The letters seemed oversized, as if they were flying straight toward Aliya. She stared at them. Something inside her shrank. But before she could delve further into her thoughts, the bus pulled into a free parking space directly in front of the arrivals terminal and came to a stop. No one said a word. The silence seemed to stretch on for an eternity for Aliya – until it was broken by Abu Khalid's powerful voice: "Hanna, Farah – you're first. You leave the bus now and go to the spot described to you in the map. Maha, you go with Yara. And Aliya – you go with Eleen. Go to the place I've assigned you as quickly and discreetly as possible. You know what happens next."

The bus door was opened from the outside by Omar. One last look back. Aliya's eyes met Latifa, who had her arm around Abu Khalid and wasn't meeting her gaze. In the cockpit, she saw three detonators, flashing green until the moment they would turn a deadly red – then the door closed.

Hanna and Farah were the first to enter the building and headed toward Terminal 3. Maha and Yara followed. They turned toward Terminal 1, while Aliya and Eleen headed toward Terminal 4. Aliya saw the many people who had gathered here early Sunday: cheerful mothers and fathers, laughing children, excited about the flight – on vacation, to see their grandparents. The shops were already open. The scent of freshly baked bread hung in the air. A long line had formed in front of a bakery – precise, disciplined, just as one would expect from the English. Aliya let her gaze wander through the crowd. Her steps became slower, more hesitant, more tentative, as if she were searching for something or someone.

"What is it, Aliya? Come on, we have to move on." Eleen was close behind her, urging her to move on. Aliya now looked around on the other side, searching, almost hoping – but she didn't find what she was looking for. Only a few more meters. Then they would reach the square. Where she would leave Eleen. Because her task would end here. And Aliya's too. Just one more minute. Maybe two. Just a few more steps and nothing would be the same – at Heathrow Airport...

Two months earlier:

Aliya was on her way back from the market. In her bag were fresh eggplants and zucchini – carefully selected for dinner the next day. Reza and Amara had announced their arrival. Aliya wanted to fill the vegetables with bulgur and serve it with a cool yogurt sauce – simple, but full of memories of the past.

She had just arrived at Reza's shop when the door opened and he suddenly stood before her. No greeting. No smile. Just a fixed stare. At the same moment, two men stepped out of the store. Without a word, they grabbed Aliya by the arms – left and right – and led her purposefully into the store.

Reza followed them. The door closed behind him. He locked it. Aliya stared at him in horror.

"What's going on, Reza? What are you doing here? Let me go immediately!"

Her voice trembled more with anger than fear. But the men didn't react. Calmly, almost mechanically, they led her to a chair and pushed her into it – not brutally, but firmly.

Reza also fetched a chair and sat down opposite her. His face was expressionless, almost tired. The two men stood to her right and left, like shadows, silent, watchful.

"Now listen to me carefully, Aliya."

Reza's voice was quiet, but every note cut clearly through the room.

"I'll say these words to you only once, and it will be your only chance."

He leaned forward slightly, looking her straight in the eyes.

"We know who you're meeting. And we know you're planning something."

Aliya stirred, about to say something – but a barely noticeable shake of Reza's head made her stop.

"We've been monitoring Latifa and her husband for several years. And we know they're preparing something big. Something very big."

He repeated the last sentence – slower. More clearly. Almost like a threat.

"Who are we?"

Aliya spoke more quietly now, but more sharply. The initial wave of panic had subsided.

"What do you know? And what's all this about?"

She looked directly at Reza. Her gaze was firm, almost defiant.

A brief moment of silence. Then Reza clasped his hands together and rested them on his knee.

"I'm laying my cards on the table now. All of them. No tricks, no double meaning. I'll tell you everything. Everything about me - who I am, who we are, and what we already know. And then... then it's your turn. Then you have a chance to tell me everything. Everything. About the plan. About Latifa. About her husband. So - are you ready? It's your only chance to get out of this whole thing. You know, I like Isa very much, and you too. We've grown fond of you both, and I don't want you to get further involved in the criminal activities of these terrorists, Aliya. You're young, you have your whole life ahead of you. Do you understand?"

Aliya nodded. Her eyes filled with tears. Undeterred, Reza continued.

"I work for the Metropolitan Police."

He said it quietly, almost casually. But it was one of those sentences after which everything changed. Forever.

"The business here..." – he made a vague gesture, as if it were all meaningless – "...just a cover. I work in a department that deals with Islamist terrorism. I monitor organized cells that shouldn't even exist, people who live in the shadows. Like your friend Latifa and her husband Abu Khalid."

The name hung in the air briefly, heavy as lead.

"We've known them for a long time. Longer than you think. We've been observing them for years. He - he stays in the background - at least so far. Intelligent, unassuming, cautious - almost like a ghost, his trail disappears every now and then. And she, she recruits new followers, exclusively women."

He paused. As if he had to sort out what he was allowed to say. Or what he finally needed to get off his chest.

"We haven't been able to prove anything against them so far. Nothing so incriminating that it would be worth arresting them. They travel to Iraq or Syria twice a year. And then they're gone, usually for about a week. Our contacts on the ground say they meet with high-ranking IS fighters there. Not just any fighters. The ones with blood on their hands. The ones with command authority."

He shook his head slightly. And then, quietly, almost to himself:

"I don't know how deep you're involved in this. Or what you thought it was. But this is definitely not a game. Not anymore."

Aliya looked at him with an expressionless face, not responding.

"We want to make you an offer," Reza gestured to the men at Aliya's side to sit down to give Aliya more room to breathe and relieve her feeling of being confined. Then he continued.

"We know about the attack on St. Paul's Cathedral, and we believe the group is behind it. We also believe they were involved in the attacks a few weeks ago - including you, Aliya."

He held Aliya's hands tightly now. Contrary to her religious beliefs, Aliya didn't pull her hands away. It was comforting to feel the gentle pressure of his hands, and it gave her a sense of security.

"We're giving you the chance to get out of this un-punished."

"What do I have to do?" Aliya's voice sounded weak.

"You have to cooperate with us, Aliya."

Suddenly, two hands landed on Aliya's shoulders and gently squeezed them. Aliya turned around and looked into Amara's eyes. It was a questioning look that said: Are you one of them too?

Amara's gaze was full of affection and hope that Aliya would be persuaded.

"We want you to tell us everything. We have evidence that the group is planning something big, something much bigger than we all believe. Something that will cost many innocent lives, and yours too, yours - Aliya. Please, work with us. Don't get drawn into something that isn't yours. Islam is a peaceful religion; don't let it be used to kill people. Don't let it take your young life away - with false promises, with false expectations."

Reza's voice had softened toward the end of his "plea," striking right at Aliya's heart, into the insecurity she'd been harbouring for weeks, into the doubts she'd been harbouring for some time.

"I'll make us some tea." Amara left the room. Aliya heard her filling the kettle and fiddling with dishes in the kitchen. They were familiar sounds. Sounds that gave Aliya a feeling of security.

Reza was now sitting quietly in front of her. He gave her the time she needed.

"Do I have to decide today?"

Her voice was quiet, almost a whisper, as if she had hoped she would be spared the answer.

"Yes," Reza answered curtly but firmly. No hesitation, no wiggle room.

She closed her eyes for a moment, took a deep breath, then it burst out.

"I'll do it. I'll help you. Just tell me what to do."

Silence. Then - almost imperceptibly - a smile flitted across Reza's face. It wasn't a simple smile. It was an expression of deep relief and genuine joy - as if he himself hadn't expected this answer.

...Aliya's eyes searched, full of panic.

"I have to leave you now."

Eleen gave Aliya a brief hug. Then she resolutely let go, turned around, and left with quick steps without looking back.

Aliya remained behind - alone, unable to move. Her body didn't move, paralyzed. She knew the belt would activate in two minutes. Two minutes - exactly from the moment Eleen left. That was how it was meant to be. That was the plan. No one came to save her, just people everywhere, trying to get to their destination quickly. Reza's plan had failed - Allah forgive me all my sins - was the last thing she thought, then two strong hands grabbed her, and Aliya lost consciousness.

"Aliya!" A voice reached her, from the distance, blurred as if through water. It slowly made its way into her consciousness, through a thicket of fog.

That voice ... she knew it. Slowly, she came to. She felt herself being carried by arms, through the crowd, experiencing a hectic commotion. Everything was bright and chaotic, yet at the same time strangely muted, as if through cotton wool.

Then – a door slam. Cool air. Light. They took her to a first-aid room and laid her carefully on a stretcher. And suddenly, everything happened very quickly.
A metallic click.
The belt was off. Just like that – gone.
And then there was Isa. He rushed to her, pulled her to him, and clutched her with a desperation that needed no words. He held her tight – so tight, as if he wanted to protect her from the whole world. And he cried. He cried uncontrollably, like someone who had

gotten back something they thought they had lost forever. Reza suddenly stepped forward from behind Isa. He smiled - calmly, relieved - and raised his thumb.

"Reza... Did everything work out? Is anyone hurt?"

"Everything went exactly as we hoped, Aliya," he replied with relief.

"We talk about everything else tomorrow, when you've recovered a bit. Now we'll take you to the hospital. Isa, you can ride with me."

Aliya was carefully carried out on a stretcher through a back entrance of the airport, away from the crowd. Only a few saw her being lifted into the ambulance. The doors closed, the blue lights flashed, and the car drove off.

It was over.

Really over.

And she was alive.

And she wanted to live - more than ever before. She wanted to experience, feel, laugh, run, and love. And she wanted to do all of that with Isa. She hadn't treated him well; he had always been so dedicated to her, and she hadn't seen it - didn't want to see it. But that would all change now. Then Aliya fell asleep from the gentle jolt of the road.

A new life

The next morning, a soft knock woke Aliya from her sleep. She blinked, opened her eyes - sterile walls, the soft beeping of a monitor. She was in the hospital.

In a weak voice, she said, "Come in."

The door opened, and Reza entered. He slowly approached her bed, pulled up a chair, and sat down next to her.

"Aliya ... I'm very proud of you," he said quietly. "You made the right decision, and you've done very well. The last few weeks must have been hell for you. You have my utmost respect for what you've done for us - for yourself."

"Reza, I'm so grateful to you." Her voice trembled slightly.

"You saved me. Truly saved me. I was about to do something unforgivable, and you stopped me. You saved my life. I was about to destroy my life, and the lives of many others."

Then she looked around the room.

"Where is Isa?"

"I sent him home so he could sleep in," Reza laughed.

"What about the other women? And do you have Latifa and Abu Khalid?"

"We stormed the bus with Latifa and Abu Khalid first. The detonators were immediately deactivated. But we didn't know if there was an automatic emergency mechanism installed on the belt - something that would have been triggered if the explosives hadn't detonated at a certain moment. So, we had to proceed with extreme caution."

Aliya looked at him with wide eyes.

"And ... what about Hanna and Yara?"

"They're both fine," Reza replied reassuringly. "We got them out of the situation just like we got you out. And we intercepted Maha, Farah, and Eleen immediately after they left you."

He paused briefly, then looked at her carefully and thoughtfully. Colour slowly returned to Aliya's face. Her shoulders slumped slightly, as if a weight had been lifted.

"Oh, Reza... I'm glad no one was hurt. What happens next?"

"There will be a trial in which you, too, will have to testify. But don't worry. I have one more piece of good news." He looked at Aliya triumphantly. "We've managed to link this planned attack and the other attacks in London to several high-ranking members of the IS leadership. The raid occurred at the same time as the one at Heathrow Airport."

"That's great, Reza!"

"We have you to thank for that, Aliya."

"I'm tired now. I'm going to sleep a little longer until Isa arrives."

Reza got up, and when he turned over again to say goodbye to Aliya, he noticed that she had already fallen asleep again.

On October 17, 2016, the major offensive to recapture the northern Iraqi city of Mosul, which had been under the control of the so-called Islamic State (IS) since 2014, began. Led by Iraqi forces, supported by Kurdish Peshmerga units, Shiite and Sunni militias,

Assyrian Christian fighters, and an international anti-IS coalition with US participation, troops advanced on the city in several waves. In January 2017, the Iraqi armed forces and their allies recaptured the eastern part of the city of Mosul. And they continued to fight bravely. After months of bitter fighting in some densely populated areas, Iraqi Prime Minister Haider al-Abadi finally announced the complete recapture of Mosul on July 9, 2017. The city had been recaptured – a symbolic turning point in the fight against IS.

Mosul, August 2019:

The sun blazed brightly in the sky, as if it were forced to show its best side. And although the people of the city were suffering greatly from the heat, the entire city was in turmoil. Since the Iraqi government officially declared the city liberated in 2018, reconstruction had been in full swing. International organizations, local aid workers, and returnees worked side by side to restore the city's devastated heart to life. A symbol of this hope was the great Al-Nuri Mosque. It had been almost completely destroyed during the fierce fighting. But now, stone by stone, its reconstruction began.

Aliya sipped her tea and placed the cup back on the small table in front of her. Satisfied, her gaze swept across the garden, which shimmered golden in the evening sun. At the far end of the garden stood the arbour, densely overgrown by two lush vines. The plump grapes hung heavy on the vines, ready for harvest. From there, the wind carried laughter - familiar, lively. She heard her father's voice, talking animatedly with Isa. Her mother sat between them, listening attentively, with that warm smile Aliya had missed so much. Rais, her little brother, was no longer a child. In the years of her absence, he had grown into a young man. This fall, he would begin his studies at the university in Mosul - he wanted to be a teacher. Aliya was very proud of him.

He was lighting the grill. They were expecting visitors that evening - Isa's family, Mariam and Muna with their husbands and children, would be coming for dinner.

Isa's gaze sought hers, a gaze full of affection. She returned it with a smile. Her hand rested on her tummy, the bulge of which was visible beneath her abaya. The twins would be born in two months – in London, where they would live together and their children would grow up.

Isa had started a position as a senior physician a few weeks ago, and they had moved into a small house in a London suburb. Reza and Amara were very excited about the new arrival – they had no children of their own. Once the children were born, Aliya's parents planned to join them in London for a few weeks. Her mother had promised to help her during the first few weeks.

Aliya leaned back. Her gaze wandered upward, to the branches of her small date tree that spread above her. It had grown considerably in recent years. She reached out, plucked a date, and put it in her mouth. It was sweet and soft – just like the dates from the market, whose pits she had once planted.

ENDE

About the author

I live with my family in the far north of Bremen. Writing is my great passion, sometimes exciting, sometimes thoughtful, but always from the heart. Whether it's a regional crime novel or current social issues such as religious conflicts, war and displacement, or personal stories – I refuse to be pigeonholed. My stories arise from what moves me.